P9-CBF-494

The
Magic Nation
Thing

ALSO BY
Zilpha Keatley Snyder

FEATURING THE STANLEY FAMILY

THE HEADLESS CUPID
THE FAMOUS STANLEY KIDNAPPING CASE
BLAIR'S NIGHTMARE
JANIE'S PRIVATE EYES

AND CONDORS DANCED
BLACK AND BLUE MAGIC
CAT RUNNING
THE CHANGELING
THE EGYPT GAME
FOOL'S GOLD
THE GHOSTS OF RATHBURN PARK
GIB AND THE GRAY GHOST
GIB RIDES HOME
THE GYPSY GAME
LIBBY ON WEDNESDAY
THE RUNAWAYS
SEASON OF PONIES
SONG OF THE GARGOYLE
SPYHOLE SECRETS
SQUEAK SAVES THE DAY
THE TRESPASSERS
THE TRUTH ABOUT STONE HOLLOW
THE UNSEEN
THE VELVET ROOM
THE WITCHES OF WORM

The Magic Nation Thing

Zilpha Keatley Snyder

Delacorte Press

Published by
Delacorte Press
an imprint of
Random House Children's Books
a division of Random House, Inc.
New York

Visit us on the Web! www.randomhouse.com/kids
Educators and librarians, for a variety of teaching tools, visit us at
www.randomhouse.com/teachers

Library of Congress Cataloging-in-Publication Data

Snyder, Zilpha Keatley.
  The magic nation thing / Zilpha Keatley Snyder.
     p. cm.
  Summary: Although twelve-year-old Abby has always tried to deny that she
has some kind of weird psychic power, she takes advantage of it to help her
mother, a struggling private investigator, and, more importantly, to find her best
friend's little brother when he goes missing at a ski resort.
  ISBN 0-385-73085-3 (trade)—ISBN 0-385-90107-0 (GLB)
  [1. Psychic ability—Fiction. 2. Private investigators—Fiction. 3. Family
life—California—San Francisco—Fiction. 4. Friendship—Fiction. 5. San
Francisco (Calif.)—Fiction.] I. Title.
  PZ7.S68522Mag 2005
  [Fic]—dc22

                                                              2004010105

Printed in the United States of America

August 2005

10 9 8 7 6 5 4 3 2 1

BVG

TO CHARLOTTE AND BROOKE THOMAS, WHO,
AS YOUNG SQUAW VALLEY SKIERS,
GAVE ME INVALUABLE ADVICE

1

NOT LONG AFTER Abigail O'Malley helped solve the Moorehead kidnapping case, a problem she'd had all her life took a definite turn for the worse. It was a personal and very secret problem that she'd never shared with anyone, not even Paige Borden, who was her best and closest friend. So embarrassingly personal, in fact, that she had never allowed herself to believe that it actually existed, at least not for sure.

Abby was twelve and a half years old when the kidnapping occurred, and in the seven years since her mother, Dorcas O'Malley, had become a private investigator, Abby had never gotten involved in any of her cases. At least not on purpose. And she had no plans to do so in the future. She had, in fact, made her feelings on the subject quite clear in an essay she'd written only a few days before Dorcas started work on the Moorehead case.

The essay was for Ms. Eldridge's seventh-grade language arts class, its title was to be "My Future Career," and it was supposed to be at least two pages long. Most of the class groaned when Ms. Eldridge gave the assignment. "Two whole pages on what you're planning to be someday? What if you haven't made up your mind?" Paige whispered.

"I thought you had," Abby whispered back, grinning. "You know. About being a movie star or a fortune-teller?"

"Don't laugh." Paige frowned. "I meant it."

Abby made her nod say "I know you did" and went back to her own list of career choices. Once she'd started, she found it wasn't so difficult after all. For one thing, she'd always been a list maker, so coming up with one of future careers was an interesting challenge. There were, she discovered, quite a few things she might want to do as an adult. But nowhere in the list was there one word about being a private investigator.

Abby's essay was going to say that her first and most important goal was to be a gold medalist in the Winter Olympics. After that, a career as either a ski instructor or a lawyer, like her father. Along with getting married and raising a big <u>normal</u> family (important word underlined). No mention of detective work.

The career choices were fairly recent, but the family thing Abby had always planned on, especially the normal part. Over the years she had changed her mind several times about future careers, starting with cowgirl when she was in kindergarten, and librarian when she began to love reading and was under the mistaken impression that all librarians had to do was sit around reading all day.

But being a private investigator had never been one of her choices. Not ever, in spite of the fact that she was the daughter of Dorcas O'Malley, who, according to Tree, was one of the best detectives in California. Or at least in northern California, where there were fewer crimes but the ones that did happen tended to be more original. That was what Tree said anyway, but then, Tree (short for Teresa Torrelli) was Dorcas's employee, and under the circumstances she'd probably felt it was the tactful thing to say.

But Abby had her own ideas about the O'Malley Detective Agency—ideas that were based on a lot more inside information. After all, Tree had been working for the agency only a couple of years, but it had been a big part of Abby's life ever since she started kindergarten. Which coincidentally was the same year her father had moved to Los Angeles and her parents got a divorce.

Before Abby's father, Martin O'Malley, moved away, the whole family, Abby and Dorcas and Martin, had lived in a great house in the Marina. But after the divorce they had to sell the house Abby had lived in since she was a baby so that Martin could pay for his apartment in Los Angeles and Dorcas could start the agency. Someone else owned the Marina house now, but Abby could still draw accurate floor plans of every room. And she still liked to look at it as they drove by and try to remember what living there had been like. Not that driving by happened all that often anymore. Not since Dorcas decided that mourning over a house wasn't a normal thing to do. Perhaps not, but to Abby's way of thinking, she'd lost a lot of other normal things right about then, and if drawing pictures of a normal house helped, she didn't see what was wrong with doing it.

After the divorce the O'Malley Detective Agency had set up shop in the two front rooms of a small shabby Victorian, and Dorcas and Abby moved into what was left over. Abby hadn't been quite six years old at the time, but she wasn't likely to forget how she'd had to practically live at Mrs. Watson's Day Care Center because of Dorcas's strange work hours. And how Dorcas had to worry all the time, not only about not getting enough clients, but also about things such as termites and leaky plumbing and unpaid bills. And Abby had to go without all kinds of things that most of the girls at her school got from their parents without even asking.

Things had been a little bit better recently, at least financially, but Abby's interest in becoming a private investigator was still pretty much nonexistent. In fact she'd told her mother so more than once, and one morning in October the subject came up again while she and Dorcas were having breakfast. At the time, they were sitting in the little breakfast nook in the practically antique kitchen (no dishwasher), and both of them were already dressed for the day: Abby in her Barnett Academy uniform, and Dorcas in a blue suit that, as usual, she'd managed to hoke up with scarves and bangles, so that the end result was something halfway between a businessperson and a gypsy palm reader. Abby was checking out all the bracelets and amulets when Dorcas asked her how she was doing on the Future Career essay.

"I have it all outlined," Abby told her mother. "But I haven't quite decided whether to work as a ski instructor for a while first, or to start right out studying for my law degree."

She was still considering what her decision would be when her mother, with a smile that was only halfway joking, said, "Oh, but I thought for sure you'd want to take over the agency someday."

Abby shrugged. "Mom. You know I just don't have any interest in that kind of thing." For years Abby had called her mother Dorcas most of the time, but now and then, often when they were arguing, the Mom word came out, usually in a tone of voice that made the point that Dorcas was being too Smothering (*mothering* with a big *S*). "At least you *should* know it," Abby added. "I've said so often enough."

"Darling"—Dorcas O'Malley reached out to pat Abby's hand—"I know. I know how you felt about me starting the agency and I know you'd much prefer to have a mother who did something . . ." She paused and her upside-down smile made it clear that what she was saying was a put-down. "Something more socially acceptable, like arranging ski trips and taking tennis lessons."

Abby was swallowing a mouthful of oat bran cereal at that moment or she might have interrupted resentfully. Dorcas was obviously putting down Daphne Borden, Paige's mom. It wasn't the first time Dorcas had used that tone of voice when talking about the Borden family. As if the Bordens were uninteresting just because they lived like they had gobs of money, which of course they did. But before Abby could get started on a suitable response, something such as "I know you think that the Bordens are boring, but I don't see what would be so boring about living in a mansion instead of the back side of a detective agency," her mother's little speech took an entirely different, but equally familiar, turn.

"About why you might consider joining the agency, Abby . . ." Dorcas's uncertain smile hinted that she knew Abby wasn't going to agree. But she went on anyway. "I do think that you have an extraordinary ability to pick up on important information that no one else might notice. Remember that time you—"

That did it. Abby knew what her mother was leading up to because she'd mentioned it so many times before. Dorcas was going to bring up a case she'd been working on a year or so before, in which this crummy guy snatched a purse from an old lady—a purse that held some papers and photos that were so important the woman hired Dorcas's agency to try to find them. And Abby had just happened to come in while she was in the office talking to Dorcas. Abby had listened to the old lady talk about her precious photos for just a couple of minutes, and a little while later she'd made a wild guess as to where the purse might be.

Finding the old woman's purse was just the result of a hunch that happened to be right, but it was enough to make Dorcas start talking about "Abigail's special gift." A gift that she supposedly inherited from some strange ancestors way back in Dorcas's family tree who could read people's minds, find missing objects, and do other weird things. And whom Dorcas had learned about when she was a child, from an old lady she called Great-aunt Fianna.

Abby didn't enjoy Dorcas's stories about her weird ancestors, particularly after she began to suspect that one of the main reasons Dorcas had decided to stay in San Francisco and be a detective instead of moving to Los Angeles and staying married was that she really believed she herself had inherited some special powers that would help her become a world-famous detective.

But the way Abby saw it was . . . Well, okay—on the one hand, having a career doing something you were extra good at *was* important, whether it was skiing or solving mysteries. But on the other hand, so was having a normal family life.

So when her mother started to bring up the purse-snatching episode, Abby wasn't exactly enthusiastic. "No," she said, shaking her head. "I didn't use any special powers when they caught that purse snatcher. I mean, that isn't the way it happened. I didn't have any supernatural vision about where that guy hid it. Like I told you, I must have just happened to think of where he might have gone right after he took the purse and—and . . ." Abby stuttered to a stop. It was a familiar discussion that had never gotten anywhere and wasn't about to now.

"All right. I'm sorry I mentioned it," Dorcas said. "I only meant to suggest that—"

"I know what you meant," Abby interrupted. "You meant you think that you—that both of us—can do weird things. Like reading other people's minds, and maybe getting mysterious, out-of-thin-air messages about who-dunit?" Twisting her mouth into a sarcastic grin, she went on, "Or how about flying around on broomsticks?"

Dorcas's exasperated sigh started out angry and wound up sounding a little bit like an apology. "I know, sweetie. I probably shouldn't have told you so much about the things Aunt Fianna used to tell me. But I do think there was some truth in her stories."

Dorcas shrugged and went on. "When I was no more

than five or six I sometimes knew what people were thinking without being told. And I could find things that had been lost for ages. And I do think some of my success as an investigator is probably due to my ability to . . ." She paused and checked out Abby's expression (which this time was probably saying something like "Not that one again") before she smiled and changed the subject. "Well, you'll have to agree that I've managed to make us a living as an investigator since your father left. I've done it all by myself, and I do feel I'm quite good at what I do."

Abby shrugged and said, "Okay, okay. I know you're a good PI, Mom. But right now I have to go get ready to catch the bus. Okay?" She left the kitchen and climbed the narrow stairs that led to her own private room, where things were arranged just the way she wanted them. Where everything—books, board games, and even the shelfful of her old outgrown toys—was lined up exactly where she had known it would be, because she herself, not anyone else—supernatural or otherwise—had put it there.

Actually there was plenty of time before she had to leave, but she had needed to get away. Sitting down at her desk, she picked up her notes for her Future Career essay and started to reread them, but her mind kept flip-flopping back to one thing in particular that had been said at the breakfast table. To one word, actually. The word *left*—as in "since your father *left*." As if the divorce had been all his idea.

Not that either of them had ever said so. Neither of them had told Abby much about why they'd gotten divorced. They'd probably thought she was too young to understand at the time, but even now that she was almost thirteen, they still wouldn't talk about it. But it had always seemed obvious to Abby that everything had been fine until her dad's firm moved him to Los Angeles and her mom chose San Francisco and her new detective agency.

As for the things that had been said at the breakfast table, there was definitely no point in trying to explain to Dorcas why Abby's idea of a *normal* family didn't include a parent who spent most of her time associating with people like purse snatchers and hit-and-run drivers instead of spending time with her family. And it certainly didn't include having weird supernatural ancestors.

That was just how she felt about the whole thing, and what happened with the kidnapped kid's locket didn't change her way of thinking one bit.

THE MOOREHEAD KIDNAPPING episode began only a
few days after Abby and her mother had had that discussion
at the breakfast table. Dorcas had just taken a case concerning a kidnapped six-year-old kid. The little girl, whose
name was Miranda Moorehead, had gone out to visit a
friend who lived right down the street—and she never got
there. Disappeared, it seemed, into thin air.

The police thought the kidnapper might be the girl's father, who was divorced from her mother and had moved to
Oregon. A father who had lost the right to see his daughter
because, according to his ex-wife, he had a mean streak and
a violent temper. But nobody knew for sure if he was the kidnapper, because he'd recently sold his house and business in
Portland and dropped out of sight. And no one, not even the
police, could find out where he'd gone. Then Mrs. Moore-

head called up and said she'd heard about the O'Malley Agency from a friend, and asked Dorcas to take the case, and Abby picked up the kitchen phone and listened in.

As a rule Abby tried not to pay any attention to the cases her mother was working on. But this case had been a little harder to ignore because it had happened so close to where the Bordens lived. And also because Paige Borden, Abby's absolutely best friend in the whole world, was sure she'd seen the victim at the supermarket a few days before the kidnapping.

According to Paige, she'd been right behind this kid and the kid's mother in the check-out line, and they'd been arguing about whether to buy some candy. The little girl kept saying, "Daddy always let me buy some." And the mother kept saying, "Miranda, please stop saying that." Paige was sure the mother had called the little girl Miranda, which, as she kept pointing out, is not a terribly common name. And later, when the *Chronicle* printed a picture of Miranda, Paige was sure she looked exactly like the girl she'd seen in the market.

That made the whole thing a little more interesting, and Abby had even gone so far as to read some of the newspaper stories about the kidnapping. It was mainly because Paige was so fascinated by the whole thing that Abby had eavesdropped when Dorcas had been talking on the phone to the kidnapped girl's mother. But that was all she'd done about it until the locket thing happened.

Dorcas had been on the Moorehead case for only a few days on the Saturday morning when Abby got involved. She might have flown down to see her dad that weekend, but he was visiting a client in New York, and as for Dorcas, there was no telling where she was. She'd made a quick trip to Portland the day before. And that day, who knew where? But Tree was supposed to be in the office that morning when Abby went in to look for a pen because all of hers had run out of ink.

Abby's pens frequently ran out of ink because of her notebook, a special loose-leaf binder that was partly a diary but also contained a large collection of lists, as well as maps and floor plans. The maps she'd drawn of her favorite places, such as the Marina and Pacific Heights and Squaw Valley, and the floor plans were of houses she'd lived in or visited. As for the diary, she'd been keeping one since she was about seven years old, and she'd started making lists even before that. Long lists of everything she did and wore and ate, of all the books she read and whether she liked them, as well as all the other things and people she especially liked or disliked. She wasn't sure why, but there was something satisfying about list keeping—even though it did use up a lot of ink.

The office of the O'Malley Agency consisted of two rooms, one of which had once been a fairly large Victorian parlor complete with high ceilings and a nice marble fireplace. But now, instead of comfortable chairs and sofas like you'd find in most people's living rooms, it held a couple of big beat-up desks, several cluttered tables, three computers, and a couple of armless chairs where clients were supposed to sit. And beyond the parlor, in what had once been a dining room, there were more cabinets and office equipment, such as copiers and fax machines. Because neither Tree nor Dorcas had much interest in unexciting housekeeping activities, the whole area also had a lot of dusty surfaces and overflowing wastebaskets.

That morning the office was, as usual, full of dust, but unusually empty of people. No Tree, that is. But the BACK IN A MOMENT sign was on the front door, which probably meant that Tree had run down to the corner grocery store to buy something for lunch.

Abby managed to find a pen on Dorcas's messy desk and was about to borrow it when she noticed a fat envelope with *Moorehead* written across the top. She didn't pick it up right away because—well, just because she wouldn't want to give anyone who happened to come in the idea that she was all that interested in one of her mother's investigations. Instead she went to the front window, where she could see if anyone was about to arrive on the scene.

It was a typical autumn day in San Francisco, clear and sunny but with a lot of wind. No dark blue Honda in the driveway, so no Dorcas. Also there was a big clue that Tree wasn't approaching at the moment: a man washing the windshield of his car right in front of the office was paying strict attention to what he was doing, which was something men hardly ever managed to do when Tree Torrelli was anywhere in the vicinity.

So the coast was clear. Abby scooted back to the desk and as she picked up the envelope some photographs fell out, and along with them a pink heart-shaped locket on a gold chain. Picking up the locket, Abby released the catch. The picture in the heart-shaped frame was obviously of Miranda herself; a larger version of the same picture had been in the *Chronicle* a day or two before. But why was the locket in the envelope? Of course Dorcas needed to know what the kid looked like, but the picture in the paper was a lot bigger and clearer.

Abby frowned as she began to understand why a locket that had belonged to Miranda was in Dorcas's file. She was remembering the Great-aunt Fianna story that had always bothered her the most: the one about how some of the strange ancestors could hold objects in their hands and get information about the people the objects belonged to. Like a message about where the owner was at that moment, or what was happening to him or her.

A special reason why that part of the weird ancestors' story made Abby particularly uneasy was that it made her wonder about something that had happened to her a lot when she was very young. But she wasn't going to let her mind go in that direction. With one side of her mouth twisted into a disbelieving smile, Abby was reaching out to put the locket back in the envelope when something strange began to happen.

The locket suddenly began to feel very warm—as warm as if it had been lying in the sun. What came next, weird as it was, wasn't an entirely new sensation. Abby remembered having that strange woozy feeling quite often when she was a little kid. The feeling that her eyes had begun to see in extra dimensions. There would be brightly colored shapes and pieces that spun around inside her head and then began to arrange themselves into patterns. One pattern and then another, until they finally came together in a real-life scene, like something in a movie. And now it was happening again. Still there, but in the shadowy distance, was Dorcas's messy desk, and behind it a dusty file cabinet, but on a closer plane a whirl of parts and pieces was quickly spinning into view.

When Abby was really young she'd kind of enjoyed the

strange sensation, as if it were her own private TV show. A show that she thought of as taking place in her Magic Nation, because that was what Mrs. Watson, the day care lady, said when Abby asked about it. "It's just your Magic Nation, dear," Mrs. Watson told her more than once. "Nothing to worry about."

So for quite a while Abby went on thinking of the experience as a visit to her Magic Nation, like Mrs. Watson said. "It's just your Magic Nation," Abby would tell herself firmly. "Nothing to worry about." And she went on not worrying about it even after she realized that what Mrs. Watson might have said was "It's just your imagination."

By the time she was nine or ten, however, Abby had started to react to the woozy feeling, and what followed it, in a different way. By then she'd begun to spend a lot of time at the Bordens' with her friend Paige, and now and then with other kids she knew from the Margaret Elston Barnett Academy, a well-known and expensive school for girls. A school that the O'Malleys never could have afforded if not for a scholarship fund that one of her father's grateful clients had set up for Abby when she was still a baby.

Most of Abby's Barnett Academy friends lived lives that were more or less like the Bordens'. Maybe a little bit less, as in having slightly smaller mansions, maybe only two or three cars instead of four, and nothing to compare to the Bordens' enormous cabin in Squaw Valley. But most of their lives were pretty much the same, with parents who had regular jobs instead of ones that required doing surveillance in Oakland one day, looking through police files in San Francisco the next, and then flying off to Portland,

Oregon, to track down a suspect the day after that. Activities that Dorcas might or might not get paid for, depending on how rich—and honest—a particular client happened to be.

As time went by and Abby became very much at home at Barnett Academy, as well as at the Bordens', she became more and more resistant to Dorcas's Great-aunt Fianna stories. And for a long time, when one of the strange visions started to happen, she would whisper, "Stop it, right this minute," put down whatever she was holding, and quickly do something to deaden her mind, like watching TV.

Now it was happening again, and as always, Abby resisted it. But even as she tried to stop it, she wasn't able to keep herself from noticing that one of the vivid scenes flashing before her eyes had formed itself into a familiar face. The smiling face of a little pigtailed girl with a missing front tooth, looking just the way she had in the newspaper picture with the article about the kidnapped kid named Miranda Moorehead.

Seeing and recognizing that face kept Abby from throwing the locket down immediately, and in that extra second or two she couldn't help zeroing in on some other things that were flashing before her eyes. Such as the fact that Miranda was starting to cry, crying hard now and pushing at something—or someone. Pushing at a large man, wearing sport shoes and a denim jacket, who was holding her by her arms and pulling her toward . . .

Toward what seemed to be a carnival ride. There was a small open vehicle, behind which a twisting metal track soared into the air. A track that was beginning to look more and more familiar. Beginning to look, in fact, exactly like the tracks of a well-known roller coaster in Disneyland. A scary roller coaster that Abby had been on more than once, and that certainly made some little kids cry when they thought about riding on it.

And then the bits and pieces that made up the roller coaster scene were blurring and fading away and a moment later reforming into . . . a smiling Miranda sitting on the shoulders of the same denim-jacketed man, who was now standing in a long line in front of what looked a lot like Mickey's House in Toontown.

When Abby dropped the locket back into the envelope, the pictures faded, and she ran away to try to put the whole thing out of her mind, not thinking about it, or at least trying not to, even though she kept remembering how hard the Moorehead kid's mother had been crying when she called Dorcas to ask her to take the case.

No one had said anything about Disneyland. Nothing at all. But Abby, who had been to Disneyland several times when she was visiting her dad in L.A., was almost sure she'd recognized some familiar Disneyland places in the scenes that had flashed before her eyes. Sitting on her bed, Abby twisted her hands together, trying to rub out the quivering, living warmth of the pink locket and at the same time wipe away the feeling that she ought to tell someone about what she'd seen—or imagined seeing.

It probably didn't mean anything, she told herself. Not anything like the possibility of Miranda being at Disneyland right at that moment. And even if it did, that didn't mean Abby ought to tell anyone about it. After all, the little girl didn't seem to be in any danger. And if the man who had taken her to Disneyland was her father, maybe it was okay that the two of them were getting a chance to spend some time together. Abby could see how that might be true. Which meant she didn't have to do something that would be as good as admitting that she, Abby O'Malley, really had inherited some weird powers from Great-aunt Fianna.

3

ABBY WAS WORKING at keeping her mind off the whole locket episode by concentrating on the tuna sandwich she was making when she suddenly realized that she ought to call Paige and ask if they could play some games on her computer or even just watch TV together for an hour or so. She wasn't going to say, "Or anything else that might help keep my mind off that stupid locket," even though that was definitely what she was thinking. So she called Paige's cell phone number and, with her mouth still full of tuna, mumbled her question about whether it was a good time for her to visit. To her immense relief, Paige said, "Sure. Come on over."

Abby swallowed hard and said, "Okay. Great. I'm on my way." All that was left to do was bolt down the rest of her lunch and leave a message with Tree, in case Dorcas got back early. And borrow a little bus money. The area where the Bordens lived was within walking distance of the O'Malley Agency if you had a lot of energy and a half hour or so to spare, but a long walk with lots of time to think was exactly what Abby wasn't interested in at the moment.

In the office Tree was at her desk finishing her lunch, some microwave-type spaghetti thing with lots of gooey tomato sauce. In spite of a mouthful of spaghetti, she managed a smile that would have looked fabulous on the cover of any fanzine. "Hi, Abbykins," she said. (Abby wouldn't have allowed anyone else to call her Abbykins, but she didn't mind when Tree did it.) "What's up?"

Abby sighed. A wishful sigh that meant *Why can't I look that good?* which was what most females thought when they looked at Tree Torrelli's naturally curly hair, enormous dark eyes, inch-long eyelashes, and figure that Paige said was "absolutely insane." Which, when Paige said it, meant like fabulous, only even better.

It was obvious that Tree hadn't combed her hair since her windy walk to the store, and strands of crispy black curls straggled around her face, besides which there was a glob of tomato sauce in the middle of her chin. Not at her best, maybe, but probably good enough to get discovered as the next Hollywood superstar if a movie scout happened to walk in. But Abby didn't say so. She'd found out a long time before that Tree didn't like people to mention her good looks, which Abby didn't understand at all until Dorcas explained it.

Dorcas said that Tree was from a large Italian family in which most of the kids got sent to college, but not Tree. Not Tree, because her family's attitude was that any girl who looked like her didn't need a career because she could just marry for money.

"Tree really resented her family's attitude," Dorcas had explained. "So she left home and worked her way through college. So if you want to compliment Tree, don't tell her she's gorgeous. I found out that if I told her she was a quick learner, or a whiz at the computer, she was absolutely thrilled. But believe me, as far as Tree Torrelli is concerned, the word *gorgeous* is a put-down."

So all Abby did was grin at Tree and say, "Hey, I called Paige and she wants to see me, so could the agency loan me some bus money?"

Tree wiped the spaghetti sauce off her big beautiful mouth, grinned back, and said, "Good idea. It's too nice a day to sit around home. I'll tell your mom when she gets in." As soon as Tree got some bus money out of petty cash, Abby was on her way to the Bordens'.

Abby always enjoyed looking at the Bordens' mansion as she walked up the hill from the bus stop. She particularly liked the grand balcony right over the front door, and the spiraling columns that held it up. A balcony that always made Abby think of the ones on which English kings and queens stood to wave to admiring crowds below.

Abby had heard Dorcas telling Tree that the Bordens' house was ostentatious, which, according to the dictionary, meant something like "overly elaborate and ornate." But Abby didn't agree at all. She couldn't see what was wrong with any of it, including the modern computer-controlled appliances and all the interior decorator–styled rooms. Particularly Paige's big beautiful bedroom with its velvet swag drapes and matching bedspread that you could barely see under all the matching velvety pillows.

As Abby walked up the broad staircase that led to the

double doors under the "royal balcony," she was remembering and resenting Dorcas's "ostentatious" remark and thinking that there were a lot of good things about the Bordens besides their house—their *houses* if you counted the one in Squaw Valley. Of course the best thing about the Bordens was Paige.

As Abby pushed the doorbell and waited for someone to let her in, she thought about how Paige had been her friend ever since second grade. Her best friend, even though in some ways they weren't that much alike. In size, for instance. Although they were almost exactly the same age, Paige was quite a bit bigger. She was taller and blond. Abby was small for her age with dark hair and eyes.

There were other differences too, such as Paige's crazy imagination, and the headlong, fearless way she did everything, which could be a little scary at times except that she always had a kind of confidence that made Abby feel she'd be able to deal with whatever mess she might get herself, and Abby, into. Abby tended to be more cautious and to worry too much about things that might happen, or might not happen the way they were supposed to. Except when they were skiing, of course. The only place where Abby was the fearless one was on the slopes.

Abby had often wished she could be more like Paige, but Paige said she envied things about Abby. "Like how you get good grades without even trying," Paige had said. "And the way you move, like a dancer or a champion athlete."

And when Abby had protested, saying she was lousy at badminton and not too great at soccer, Paige had interrupted to say, "Well, a champion skier anyway. You know you are. Everybody says so. Or even a champion figure skater, if you'd had a chance to work at it a little more when you were young."

So that was Paige, and as for the rest of the Borden family . . . Well, Daphne, Paige's mom, had been the one who'd persuaded Dorcas to start letting Abby go with the Bordens to their Squaw Valley cabin. And she told everyone how much Paige's skiing had improved since she'd had someone her own age to ski with.

When it came to Sherwood Dandrige Borden II, Paige's father (Sher for short, pronounced like *sure*), Abby didn't have as much to go on, since he usually wasn't home when she was there. But at Squaw he'd always been nice enough, as long as everybody obeyed the rules.

Of course Paige griped about both of her parents a lot. Especially about how her dad never listened to her when she complained about her brothers. But she did seem proud of some things about her mom and dad. Things such as knowing what was the best stuff to buy and, of course, being *such* expert skiers.

Abby pushed the doorbell again and went on thinking about how much she liked the Bordens. All of them, even Sky and Woody, despite the fact that she was, at that very moment, standing in the *very* spot where she'd been hit by an egg that Sky had dropped from the balcony. Abby glanced up and was moving out of egg range when the door opened and there they were, both of them.

Six-year-old Skyler Hardison Borden, known as Sky, was pointing his favorite toy, a water gun shaped like an Uzi, at Abby's midsection. Behind him was eight-year-old Woody, whose full name was Sherwood Dandrige Borden

III. Woody the Third wasn't carrying a gun, but with the fiendish grin on his face, karate outfit, and kickboxer pose, he really didn't need a weapon.

Abby grinned, which as usual seemed to take both of them by surprise. "Hi, guys," she said, getting ready to duck back out of reach in case Sky started to pull the trigger. "Where's Paige?"

Skyler turned to look at Woody, who slashed the air with both hands and then struck a different karate pose before demanding, "Who wants to know?"

Narrowing her eyes and cupping her hands around her mouth, Abby whispered, "The FBI." As Woody thought that over she pushed past him just as Paige came running down the stairs. Ignoring her warlike siblings, Paige grabbed Abby's arm and pulled her away. "Come on in," she said. "Sky, if you shoot that thing off on Mom's Persian carpet you're going to get killed."

As Abby and Paige ran up the stairs, Skyler shouted after them, "No, I'm not. You are. You're going to get killed." But Paige only laughed and went on running.

ONCE INSIDE PAIGE'S interior-decorated room, Abby and Paige flopped down on the ankle-deep champagne-colored throw rug and talked. For a while they talked about clubs. Lately there had been a fad at school of making up secret clubs that no one except the club members were allowed to be in, or even know about.

"We ought to have one," Paige said. "We could call it the P and A Club, for Paige and Abby. And we'll have more secrets than anyone."

"Okay," Abby said. "What kinds of secrets shall we have?"

Paige thought for a minute before suggesting that they could have secrets about the fact that they were both adopted and their real parents had been wizards. Paige had been reading Harry Potter recently.

After they'd decided a lot of stuff about what had happened to their real parents and how they'd ended up living with Muggles, they switched to making up secret clubs for some of their classmates. They decided, for instance, that Margot and Heather should start a secret club called the Barnett Pets, which you couldn't join unless you were the teacher's pet in most of your classes.

In between making up clubs, they played a new computer game that Paige said was really insane (fabulous, that is), even though it seemed to be a lot like most of the other games they'd played recently. And then, wouldn't you know it, Paige brought up the one subject Abby didn't want to think about.

"Does your mother have any new clues about what happened to Miranda? You know, my mom says what probably happened was that she got into a car with a stranger. My mom says that's usually how people get kidnapped. They get into a car with a stranger and that's the last they're ever heard of." Paige's blue-green eyes tipped mournfully. "I've just been worried to death about that poor little girl. It's so much worse when something like that happens to someone you know." Paige liked to make it sound as if the Moore-heads were old friends of the family instead of some people she'd possibly seen once in a grocery store check-out line.

Abby shook her head. "No new clues that I know about. But my mom flew up to Oregon yesterday, so she must still be thinking Miranda might be up there with her father. That's all I know," she added firmly. On one hand she really wanted to tell Paige about the locket, but on the other hand she knew she'd better not.

The problem with telling Paige about the locket, or anything having to do with secret powers, was that Abby knew she'd be totally fascinated. Paige's interest in anything weird and scary was one of the few areas where she and Abby disagreed. Abby felt pretty certain that once she started the locket story, she would wind up telling way too much. Such as all about Great-aunt Fianna and the other weird ancestors and about how Dorcas seemed to think that she, and maybe Abby too, had inherited something that Dorcas referred to as psychic abilities. Abilities that Abby would be glad to trade in any day for a nice ordinary life with parents who lived in Pacific Heights and talked about normal things like golf scores and when to go on their next ski trip instead of who did what and whether it was a crime.

So Abby changed the subject back to how much one computer game could be just like five or six others. After that there was a long monologue by Paige about how lucky Abby was not to have any little brothers. Apparently it had been a particularly bad day for Paige, little brother–wise, and she told Abby about it in detail.

The worst part of the story was about how Sky had gotten into her makeup that morning while she had been out shopping with her mother. Paige had a great cosmetic kit with just about every kind of makeup you could imagine. Even things like glitter eye shadow and glow-in-the-dark lipstick. So far she hadn't been allowed to wear any of it, except on Halloween, but she was saving it for the future, in a box at the back of her closet.

"When we got home Sky had lipstick and rouge all over his face," she told Abby. "Of course he had to scrub it off as soon as Mom saw him. But he'd already messed up some of my best stuff, and then Mom took the rest of it."

"All of it?" Abby asked.

"Well, all but one icky pink lipstick," Paige said.

"What did she do with it?" Abby wanted to know. "Did she throw it away?"

"No, I guess not. But she might as well have. She said she was putting it away until I was older." Paige shrugged. "Like twenty-one probably."

"That's awful." Abby was sympathetic, but she couldn't help grinning. "Now that you mention it, I did notice that Sky looked even cuter than usual. It must have been your makeup."

"Sky is a monster," Paige snorted. "They both are. But Sky's the worst because he gets away with murder because of the way he looks. I mean, who else could go around looking angelic while he's carrying an Uzi?" She sighed. "You'd think they could have settled for one. After they got their Sherwood Dandrige the Third, you'd think that would have been enough. But no, they had to go on and have another one. I mean, Woody would have been majorly monstrous all by himself, but having Sky to show off for just makes him a thousand times worse."

Abby thought calling your little brothers monstrous was a bit harsh, but she could understand Paige's point of view. And it was certainly true that Sky in particular got away with everything just by being cute. So darling that adults meeting him for the first time tended to make that *ahhh* noise that's often used for puppies or kittens. And like puppies and kittens, Skyler Borden got away with almost anything—including dropping eggs on people who came to the front door.

"My mom and dad knew he did it," Paige had told Abby

28

after the egg attack. "They yelled at him a little but it was like they really thought it was kind of amusing. And of course, he knew they felt that way."

"I know," Abby told Paige. "It doesn't seem fair. It really doesn't."

By the time Abby finished sympathizing, it was time for her to head for home—and on the way try to keep her mind on computer games and little brother problems instead of letting it slide toward Disneyland and who might be there.

Dorcas got home soon after Abby did, and at dinner that night (the usual microwave stuff), she didn't bring up the Moorehead case or what she'd been doing about it. Abby had kind of been hoping she would, hoping Dorcas might mention that she'd been thinking about where a kidnapping father might have taken his six-year-old daughter if he was trying to get her to be on his side. But no such luck.

All during dinner Dorcas talked only about a phone call she'd just had with Abby's dad about what kind of new car she ought to buy if and when she got enough money saved up. Even though they were divorced, they were still good enough friends for her to ask Abby's dad's advice about something every few days. But this time she hadn't agreed with his suggestion.

As usual, Abby was on her dad's side. Not that she knew much about cars, but she was almost always on her dad's side about almost everything. Particularly when the argument seemed to be about whether Dorcas ought to sell the agency and go back to being a secretary and housewife. Not that Martin ever came right out and said exactly that, but there were times when it seemed to Abby that he was getting pretty close.

Abby was having trouble concentrating on the new-car discussion because she kept thinking about the Miranda problem. After a while she even did something she'd never done before and really didn't want to try because if it worked, it might mean that Dorcas was right about the weird powers thing.

What she did was try to give her mother a kind of mental push in the right direction by concentrating on Miranda and Disneyland—an effort that required staring at Dorcas's forehead, shutting everything else out of her mind, and thinking, Miranda's in Disneyland, Miranda's in Disneyland, over and over again. Okay, maybe a little like mental telepathy, which Abby didn't believe in either but under the circumstances might be worth a try. Or maybe not, because it didn't work. Dorcas didn't get the message.

That would have been the end of it, except that Abby kept remembering, in fact almost hearing like an echo, how Mrs. Moorehead had cried when she'd talked about missing her little girl. At last, when Dorcas had almost finished her ice cream, Abby decided to take a more direct approach by asking, "Anything new about the Moorehead kidnapping?"

It wasn't a typical question for Abby to ask, and Dorcas looked at her sharply. "Not really," she said. "The leads in Portland have pretty much fizzled out." She stared at Abby with a thoughtful expression on her face. "Why?" she asked finally. "Why do you ask?"

Abby's first inclination was to shrug and change the subject, but then she heard it again, the echo of sobbing, and she found herself saying, "I was just thinking that if it *was* Miranda's father who kidnapped her, maybe he'd try to take her someplace fun. You know, so at the next custody hearing she'd tell her mother and the judge that she wanted to be with her dad."

Dorcas was listening very carefully. "Someplace fun?" she asked. "Like . . . ?"

Now Abby shrugged elaborately. "Oh, I don't know. To the beach maybe, or the zoo, or . . ." She paused and then, as if she'd just thought of it, "Or maybe someplace like Disneyland."

"Well," Dorcas said. "I don't think a trip to Disneyland would do much to change a judge's decision, but it's something to think about." And apparently she did think about it while they were cleaning up the kitchen, because right afterward she went into the office and made a phone call. Abby tiptoed after her as far as the door, and by opening it just a crack she was able to hear a part of the conversation. Only a part, but enough to let her know that Dorcas was calling Mrs. Moorehead.

Abby was in her room reading a book, or pretending to, when the door opened and Dorcas came in looking . . . well . . . if not excited, something pretty close to it. "Abby," she said. "I've just been talking to Mrs. Moorehead."

Abby tried to look surprised. "Oh yeah?" she asked. "What about?"

"Well, concerning your idea about where Miranda and her father might be. And . . ." Dorcas paused, and the way she was staring at Abby got even more intense. "And it seems that Miranda is absolutely mad about Disneyland. She was there for the first time about a year ago and according to her mother she's scarcely talked about anything else since. It hadn't occurred to Mrs. Moorehead before, but when I suggested it, she thought that taking Miranda there might be just the kind of crazy, off-the-wall thing her ex-husband would do."

Abby nodded slowly, struggling with a confused mixture of feelings. She couldn't help being glad that Miranda might be found because of something she had done. But she didn't want Dorcas, or anyone else, to think she'd done it by using weird supernatural powers. "It was just a hunch," she said. "That's all. Just a hunch."

By early the next morning Dorcas was on a plane to southern California, and the Anaheim police as well as the clerks at all the Disneyland hotels had pictures of Miranda and her father. And within a few days the case was closed, Miranda was home with her mother, and the O'Malley Detective Agency received a lot of good publicity.

But Abby O'Malley's problem had started to take a turn for the worse.

5

RIGHT AFTER THE Moorehead kidnapping case was solved, Abby's life became even more hectic and unpredictable. What made the difference was probably the story in the *Chronicle* that mentioned that the O'Malley Detective Agency had helped the police solve the case. Of course, having a bunch of new clients was a real plus for Dorcas, and for Tree as well. But for Abby it just added to her problems. With the agency doing better, Dorcas was even busier and Abby's life got more disorganized, not to mention quite a bit lonelier.

She complained about it to her dad the next time she saw him. He was in San Francisco for a meeting and he picked her up after school. They'd stopped off for ice cream and were on their way home when she finished her sad story by saying, "I guess I ought to be glad about all the new clients, because *they* sure are. Both of them."

"Tree too?" her dad asked.

"Oh yeah," Abby said. "With Mom getting so many new cases, Tree's doing more casework, which is what she wanted to do all along. She's really happy about it."

"But you're not?"

"Well, I used to be able to at least count on Tree being there in the house every afternoon when I came home from school. And on some weekends too, when she came in to work on the Internet courses she needed for her detective's license. But now someone comes in from the steno pool to do office stuff. And they usually have to leave before Mom gets home."

Her dad waggled his bushy eyebrows and grinned at her. "So, you want to come live with me, kid?" Abby thought Dad's teasing smile made him look like a Disneyland pirate, but a good-natured one with nice gray eyes. She grinned back because they both knew he wasn't serious.

"Mom would have a fit," Abby said. Which was true. But of course there was more to it than that, and they both knew it. There would be having to say good-bye to the academy, which really was a great school, and, most important of all, to her friendship with Paige.

"Well, I'll talk to your mom about it," her dad said, and he did, but by that time the problem had been solved. And it was Daphne Borden who'd solved it.

When Mrs. Borden heard about how Abby was spending so many after-school hours all by herself, she suggested that Abby come home with Paige and wait until either Dorcas or Tree was back at the house. That was fine with Abby, Paige seemed to agree, and Dorcas said, "Daphne Borden is a good-hearted woman." And for once she didn't say it in that put-down tone of voice.

So starting in November, Abby took the Pacific Heights bus with Paige every day and usually stayed at the Bordens' until five-thirty or six. The arrangement seemed to please everyone, except maybe Woody and Sky. But then again, maybe they enjoyed the situation too, since it gave them an extra victim for their evil schemes. It wasn't long, however, before something happened that began to change the little-brother problem for the better, at least where Sky was concerned. That was when Abby rescued him from being skinned alive by Ludmilla.

Ludmilla was the enormous woman with bulgy eyes, extra-large teeth, and hulk-sized hands and feet who did the cooking at the Bordens'. Family meals usually, but she could also prepare fancy banquets for important guests when necessary. She was such an excellent cook that all of the Bordens' socially active friends said they envied the family their marvelous chef. But what the friends didn't realize was that everyone, including Sherwood Dandrige Borden II, Paige's big old businessman father, was afraid of Ludmilla.

Abby wasn't sure why. Maybe it was just because the grown-ups were afraid of losing such a fantastic cook. Paige's theory was that Ludmilla could give people the evil eye. Abby didn't take the evil eye theory very seriously, but she had noticed that no one in the family displeased the cook if they could help it.

And as for Skyler, it was pretty obvious that Ludmilla scared him to death. According to Paige, Skyler was usually his charming self during meals—throwing olive pits and pretending to barf if he saw someone eating something he didn't like. But whenever the cook came into the room, he changed completely. As long as Ludmilla was stomping around the table, Paige said, Sky was stiff and silent. So petrified he seemed unable to blink or even to swallow what was in his mouth. "He's like a zombie," Paige giggled as she told Abby, "like a scared-stiff zombie. It *must* be the evil eye. I mean, what else could do that to a monster like Sky?"

On a Wednesday afternoon something happened that really changed Sky's life. Paige's mom called to say she would be late coming home from her tennis lesson, and with their afternoon babysitter already gone, and Ludmilla not due for almost an hour, the Borden kids were more or less on their own—a rare situation that apparently inspired Woody and Sky to raid the kitchen. They were pawing through the refrigerator looking for a snack, or maybe another egg to drop on somebody's head, when Ludmilla arrived early.

What happened, according to Woody's subsequent confession, was that he and Sky heard Ludmilla's big feet stomping down the hall, and while they were scrambling to put things back where they'd found them, somebody spilled a big pitcher of orange juice. The juice ran down all over everything, through all the refrigerator shelves, and onto the floor. When Ludmilla thundered into the room, Woody, who could run faster, got away, but Sky didn't.

Abby and Paige had just arrived from school and were starting work on a math assignment when suddenly Woody burst into the room with a strangely unwarlike expression on his face.

"Hey, Woody, what's up?" Paige asked cautiously.

Woody didn't answer, but Abby was getting the impression that his intentions were somehow different than usual.

"Well, say something," Paige said. "Don't just stand there looking stupid."

That snapped Woody out of it. He made a gargoyle face by pulling down the corners of his eyes, pushing up on his nose, and sticking out his tongue, and started out of the room. But Abby was left with a strange feeling. It wasn't visual like the Magic Nation thing, but it certainly wasn't quite normal. What it felt like was . . . sheer terror. Hair-raising, skin-tingling terror that came to her not because something was threatening her, but as a faint echo of another person's fear. An echo that came from not far away and was getting stronger every second.

"Woody?" she heard herself asking, without really having known she was going to say it. "Woody, where's Sky?"

But the door had slammed and Woody was gone. Abby quickly pushed back her chair and got to her feet.

"What is it?" Paige stood up too. "Where are you going?"

"I'm not sure," Abby said. "I just think we'd better find out what's happening to Sky."

Paige snorted. "Why should I care what's happening to that little monster?" She picked up her pencil and bent her head over the math assignment.

"Yeah, okay," Abby said, "but I think I'll just go downstairs for a minute. Want to come along?"

But Paige was already engrossed in what she was doing. "Uh-uh." She shook her head. "Not right now."

So Abby went down the back stairs, and as she went, the waves of fright got stronger and clearer. The rushing current chilled her skin, throbbed in her ears, and smelled of salty tears. She kept going until she reached the kitchen door, where fear surged out around her like a silent scream. As she pushed the door open, the first thing she saw was a huge shapeless blob on the floor in front of the refrigerator. A blob that turned out to be Ludmilla down on her hands and knees mopping up orange juice.

And against the counter, sitting stiffly on a three-legged stool, was a small inconspicuous shape—a quieter, paler version of the usually only-too-noticeable Skyler Borden. One quick glance at Sky's face told Abby whose fear she had been sensing.

"Oh. Hi, Ludmilla," Abby said. "What's happening?"

Ludmilla slowly pulled her head and shoulders out of the refrigerator, and as she wrung a stream of orange juice out of her cleaning rag, she said, "This young zentleman and his brozzer have just made a zhambles of my keetchen. An absolute zhambles."

Noticing how hard it was for Ludmilla to reach the back of the refrigerator, Abby said, "Can I help? Here, let me do that."

Ludmilla lunged to her feet and then stood silently while Abby crawled halfway into the oversized refrigerator and finished mopping up the orange juice. It took a while. Ludmilla kept handing her clean rags and urging her to go over everything again. But when the orange juice was finally gone, Ludmilla went on watching while Abby walked over to Sky. Abby could feel Ludmilla's eyes boring into her back as she lifted Sky off the stool, and for that moment she almost believed Paige's evil eye theory. But to Abby's surprise, Ludmilla didn't say anything or try to keep the two of them from leaving the room.

Outside in the hall, Sky held Abby's hand for quite a while. The color of his face was becoming a little more normal, but he still didn't seem quite himself. She was curious. Squeezing his hand reassuringly, she asked, "Sky, why were you sitting on that stool?"

Sky gulped before he said in a shaky whisper, "She did it. She put me up there."

"Okay. But why did you stay there?"

"She said I had to. And . . . she said she was going to zkin me alive."

Abby couldn't help smiling. "What makes you think she'd do that?" she asked.

"Because she said so," Sky said, staring up at Abby with huge unblinking eyes.

Abby hid another smile and started to explain that when people say they're going to skin someone alive, they usually don't mean it. At least not literally. But then, looking down at Skyler's wide blue eyes, trembling lips, and small clinging hand, she thought better of it. Some six-year-old boys, she decided, were a lot more charming scared than not.

"That's okay," she told him. "I don't think she's going to skin you alive. Not today anyway."

One good consequence of the orange juice disaster was that even after Skyler got over his fright, he continued to behave differently around Abby. The very next day, in fact, he warned her that Woody had written a nasty letter on Paige's computer and signed it with Abby's name. Abby appreciated the warning, even though after she read the message she knew Paige wouldn't have been fooled for a minute. The letter read *Deer Page, I wish you were ded. Aby.*

Although what happened that day definitely changed some things for the better, it left behind something new for Abby to worry about. Like, for instance, did it mean that she had read Sky's mind, and did that mean Dorcas was right about the abnormal things she and Abby might have inherited? Those were questions Abby wasn't sure she wanted answered, but she went ahead and checked them out anyway. But after she'd tested her mind-reading powers several times on different people, she pretty much stopped worrying. When she tried to guess what Dorcas or Tree or Paige was thinking—and then asked them—she didn't come close even once. Just your imagination, she told herself. Nothing to worry about.

ON THE FIRST Saturday in November, Abby made break-fast and took a plateful of pancakes to Tree in the office. Tree, who was there to catch up on her secretarial work, was really enthusiastic. Licking her syrupy fingers, she told Abby she'd overslept and had to skip breakfast. "No time even for a cup of coffee," she said. "Or to put on my makeup." She grinned, pointing at her face. "Didn't you notice?"

Abby checked her out and said she hadn't, which was the truth. Even without makeup Tree looked better than your average female would after a week at a beauty spa. But Abby knew better than to say so.

"Well, how's the snoop business going?" she asked. "How many cases are you working on now?"

Tree grinned ruefully. "Well, your mom had me doing

surveillance on that fire insurance case. But I guess I didn't do too well."

"Oh yeah," Abby said. "I heard Mom talking to Dad about that." What she'd heard was Dorcas on the phone to Abby's dad, telling him about a new case that involved a fire in a vacant apartment building. The fire had started in a rather run-down neighborhood where there had been two other recent fires, and the insurance company thought that an arsonist must be at work. The insurance company was investigating, but it had been Mr. Barker, the owner of the third burnt-out building, who had hired the O'Malley Agency. He'd come into the office and told Dorcas that he wanted her to put someone in the neighborhood to look for any kind of suspicious behavior. So Dorcas gave Tree her first surveillance assignment.

It had been Tree's idea to start out by borrowing a friend's dog so that she could pretend to be somebody from the neighborhood out walking her dog, while she got acquainted with the area.

"The dog-walking thing seemed like a good idea," Dorcas told Abby's dad, "but the trouble with Tree doing any kind of surveillance is that she's entirely too noticeable."

Abby could guess what Tree's problem had been, but she wanted to get Tree's take on the situation. "So why do you think you didn't do a good job?" she asked. "I thought your idea about pretending to be a dog walker was a good one."

"I know. I did too," Tree said. "But it didn't work too well."

Abby could imagine. Before she'd been around the block twice, Tree had probably had dozens of guys following her around trying to make a date.

"Well . . ." Abby walked around Tree's chair, thinking and nodding. "Maybe I could help. Mom has a bunch of stuff in the attic that she uses sometimes when she doesn't want to be recognized. I'll go see what I can find."

Not much later Tree Torrelli was wearing a wig of straggly gray hair, and some "little old lady"–type shoes. Her Miss America figure was hidden under a lot of padding and a dress that looked as if it had been snatched from a bag lady's cart. Abby approved. "Now you just need some big dark glasses and maybe smudge some eye shadow on your cheeks and hands." She walked around Tree one more time and pronounced her camouflage a success. "Great," she told Tree. "Nobody would look at you twice."

Abby was still hanging around the office when Dorcas's Honda pulled into the driveway. Tree jumped up and was starting to take off the wig when Abby stopped her. "No, don't." Abby pulled Tree to the chair clients usually sat in. "There. Just sit here and let's see what happens."

Tree seemed uncertain. She started to get up twice and then sat back down, and she was doing it again when Dorcas came into the office. Dorcas nodded at Tree, said hi to Abby, and, turning back to Tree, started to say, "Hello. I'm Dorcas O'Malley. Did you want to . . ." Then she did a double take and started to laugh. Tree laughed too, and so did Abby.

"Yeah," Abby managed to say between giggles. "It was my idea. What do you think?" Apparently what Dorcas thought was that the disguise solved the "too noticeable" problem pretty well, because after she stopped laughing, she agreed to give Tree some more time on the arson case. "Dressed like that you could spend several days in the area without anybody being the wiser. Just another harmless old bag lady."

After Dorcas went out, Abby congratulated Tree for being back on the job and Tree thanked Abby for helping with the disguise. Abby could tell how eager Tree was to be the one who solved the arson case.

"I'm going to keep my fingers crossed day and night for you to be the one to solve the case," Abby said, letting her smile say that she was halfway joking. But Tree's answering grin wasn't halfway.

Giving Abby a quick hug, she said, "Thanks, Abbykins. I'll be counting on that."

So Abby crossed the two first fingers on her left hand and tried to keep them crossed constantly, and she did remember to, most of the time. But it was the crossed-fingers promise that caused a big problem.

After school on Monday, Abby and Paige were on the bus to the Bordens' when Abby realized she'd been forgetting to keep her fingers crossed. So she quickly did it, all eight fingers, two crosses on each hand, to make up for all the hours she'd forgotten. She didn't do it noticeably at all, just down in her lap, halfway under her notebook, but Paige noticed. Paige was like that. Nothing the least bit sneaky ever got past her, which probably came from all the years she'd been on the alert for little-brother surprise attacks.

Poking Abby, Paige said, "Okay. What is that for? Why did you cross all your fingers just now? Do you always do that when we're almost to my house? I'll bet you do, and I can guess why."

Abby laughed. "I'll bet you're wrong, but what's your guess? Tell me."

44

Paige smiled in the lopsided way that usually meant there was an unfunny part to what she was going to say. "I'll bet it's because of my darling little brothers." She pointed at the crossed fingers on Abby's right hand. "Like, that one's saying, 'Please, no egg on my head today.'" And then, pointing to the other hand, she said, "'And no catsup in my backpack.'"

Abby laughed and said, "Yeah, right! But no, not really. It's for Tree." And then, before she had time to bite her tongue, she went on. "I promised to keep them crossed for her to be the one to nab the arsonists."

"Arsonists. Really?" Paige's blue-green eyes went neon bright, as they always did when anything mysterious or slightly gross came up. Paige was really into stuff like that. So then of course Abby had to tell all about Tree's problems with her first surveillance assignment, and how she was trying again dressed as a bag lady. Paige thought Abby's idea to disguise Tree as a bag lady was "absolutely insane." Which meant she liked it a lot.

Paige had met Tree only a few times but she had been super impressed. Which was to be expected, since Paige was so into noticing the way people looked. She was the one who'd said that Tree had an insane figure, and that her face was a combination of Jennifer Lopez and the Olsen twins.

"So, do you think the disguise is going to work?" Paige asked eagerly. "Do you think she'll catch the arsonists?"

"Only if she's lucky," Abby sighed. "At first I thought the bag lady thing was a good idea, but now I'm not so sure. I mean, no one is going to start a fire or do anything suspicious while someone's around, even if it's just an old bag lady."

"Well, how do detectives usually do it? Do that survey . . . whatever you call it?"

"Surveillance," Abby said. "Well, sometimes they sit in a car like they're waiting for someone. Or if there's an empty apartment nearby, they rent it for a few days and sit in a window with some binoculars. Or they pretend to be workers doing something in the area. Like fixing phone lines or weeding a garden. My mom has a couple of guys she hires to do things like that."

Paige thought for a minute. "Well, I think we ought to help," she said. "I don't think we could make anyone believe we're phone repair people or gardeners. But maybe we could."

"Wait a minute—" Abby tried to interrupt, but Paige went right on.

"I know. We could take a soccer ball and pretend we're just kids practicing for a big soccer game. I think that's a great idea. Don't you?"

Abby shook her head. "No. I don't think so. Your parents would never let you hang out in that part of town and my mom wouldn't let me either."

Paige sighed and nodded slowly. "No, I suppose they wouldn't." She grinned slyly. "At least not if they knew about it. But what else can we do? Think of something."

Nothing sensible had come to mind by the time the bus reached their stop, but when Abby started to get up, Paige pulled her back down. "Wait," she said. "Sit down. This bus goes to Van Ness. If we stay on for a few more blocks we'll be almost there."

"No. We can't do that," Abby protested. "How can we? And besides, where are we going to get a soccer ball?"

"You're right." Paige frowned. "So there goes the soccer-playing idea." Then her eyes got that neon glow again. "But I have some chalk in my backpack. If anyone starts getting suspicious we can draw some hopscotch squares and start hopping."

It was a ridiculous idea, but Paige wouldn't turn loose of it, or of Abby's arm, until the doors closed and the bus was on its way. And many blocks later, with Abby still arguing and holding back, Paige pulled her down the aisle and off the bus. They hadn't walked far before they came to an area jam-packed with three-story apartment buildings, between occasional liquor stores and small take-out cafés. Not many people were on the sidewalk, and the few who were didn't look too reassuring. But Paige didn't seem aware that she and Abby might be getting into trouble.

"All right," she said in a businesslike tone of voice. "Now, this is the right area, isn't it? Exactly where were the fires?"

"I don't know," Abby said. "My mom didn't mention any exact addresses. She just said they were in this area."

"Well, come on," Paige said. "Let's start walking and maybe we'll see some burned buildings. And if anyone looks suspicious we'll start playing hopscotch."

As nervous and upset as she was, Abby couldn't help admiring Paige's courage—if that was the word for it. Courage maybe, or else just plain ignorance. Abby checked out how confidently Paige was marching along. It was as if people like Paige were so used to having things go the way they wanted them to, they just couldn't believe that anything bad might happen to them. Not even when what looked like serious trouble was just ahead. A group of guys, tough-looking characters, were standing on a street corner in front of a liquor store, and some of them stopped talking to stare at Abby and Paige as they walked by. Grabbing Paige's arm, Abby whispered, "Come on, let's go back to the bus stop. They're staring at us."

But Paige kept walking. "Why should they be staring?" she said. "We're just two girls on our way home from school. There must be lots of kids who live around here coming home from school this time of day."

"Oh sure," Abby said. "In Barnett Academy uniforms? I don't think so."

Paige glanced at her monogrammed blue blazer and pleated skirt. "Well, maybe not," she said. "I didn't think about the uniform." She slowed down and looked around just as they passed a corner where a bunch of boys were hanging out across the street. Teenage guys, maybe, with baggy pants and tight T-shirts and wide grins that somehow didn't look particularly friendly. As Abby and Paige started up the block, several of them yelled comments that Abby couldn't quite hear, or at least tried not to. Part of the threat was just things you could see, like squinty eyes and jutting chins. But what Abby couldn't shut her mind to were some silent messages that seemed more dangerous than anything that could be said out loud.

Pulling Paige to a stop, Abby turned to look back the way they'd come, back to the bus stop, where they might . . . But then some of the baggy-pants guys started crossing the street, blocking off the only route back to Van Ness and the next bus.

And now Paige finally began to get the picture. "What

do you think we should we do?" Her voice had lost its confident ring. "Run?"

"I don't think so." Something told Abby that running at that point would be almost like asking to be chased. And there was no hope that they could outrun teenage guys. She was whirling around, desperately searching for she didn't know what, when she saw up ahead, halfway up the next block, a stooped gray-haired figure in a baggy dress, moving slowly in their direction. An old homeless lady—or Tree Torrelli?

7

A FEW STEPS more and Abby was sure that what looked like a bulgy old lady with a dog on a leash really was Tree. Grabbing Paige's hand, she pulled her forward. "No, don't run," she said. "Just walk fast. And when we get there pretend you don't know her. Pretend we just want to pet her dog."

"Get where?" Paige sounded slightly frantic now. "What dog?"

"That old lady with the dog," Abby said, pointing.

Looking in the direction Abby was pointing, Paige said, "Oh, her. But how can she help? How can one old bag lady . . . ?" She glanced over her shoulder to where at least a half dozen guys were moving toward them, their slow, swaggering saunter becoming faster and more purposeful.

"No. Not a bag lady," Abby told her. "It's Tree."

"Tree?" Paige stared and then delightedly started to wave. "Tree . . . ," she was shouting when Abby grabbed her arm and whispered fiercely, "Shhh." There was a creak to Abby's voice as she said, "We have to act like we don't know her. So we don't give away her disguise."

Paige nodded uncertainly. "But what . . . ? How can she make those guys leave us alone if they think she's just an old homeless woman?"

"I don't know," Abby said desperately. "But remember, don't act like you know her. Just pretend we want to pet her dog. If we're lucky maybe those guys won't bother us with somebody right there watching."

But then Tree raised her head and saw Abby and Paige walking toward her, and just behind them a circle of teenage guys. A threatening circle that got tighter and louder until suddenly Tree stood up straight, snatched off her gray wig, and, reaching into her bag lady–type canvas purse, pulled out a pen and a small black notebook.

"All right," she said in a sharp, official-sounding tone of voice. "You boys want to give me your names?" Pointing at the nearest kid, a big overgrown hulk with a lot of gold chains around his neck, she demanded, "You first. Your name and address?" The kid stared goggle-eyed. "Why? Who . . . ," he stammered. "Who're you?"

"You want to see my badge?" Tree's voice snapped angrily. The kid shrugged, turned, and walked away. And the others did too, scattering in every direction.

On the walk to Tree's car, Paige talked a lot, telling Tree how they had been planning to help her, and how grateful they were that she'd been able to scare off the gang of toughs by pretending she was an undercover policewoman. Tree didn't say much and Abby could guess how she felt about having to blow her disguise to rescue them.

"I guess your disguise won't work anymore," Abby said ruefully.

Tree shrugged, raising her wing-shaped eyebrows. "I don't suppose so," she said. "It will probably take about ten minutes for it to be all over the neighborhood that the old bag lady with the dog is really some sort of undercover police."

Paige gasped and said, "Oh, I didn't think about that. I'm sorry. We just wanted to help and instead we messed everything up." Grimacing, she turned to look at Abby and then looked quickly away. "It was my fault," she told Tree. "Abby said we shouldn't come down here but I wouldn't listen to her."

One of the things Abby liked about Paige was that when one of her ideas didn't work too well, which happened quite a lot, she never tried to put the blame on someone else. And what she had said was true. It hadn't been Abby's fault. Except in a way it was. She should have tried harder to talk Paige out of doing such a crazy thing. The rest of the walk to the parking garage and the ride to the Bordens' house in Tree's car was pretty uncomfortable, and Paige was still apologizing when she got out of the car.

Back at the agency Tree went to get cleaned up and Abby sat in the office feeling bad and wishing there was some way she could make it up to Tree. But then Tree came back dressed in her own clothes and looking a little tired, but otherwise as gorgeous as ever.

"Look," she said. "It's okay. I don't blame you. I probably couldn't have used the bag lady disguise much longer anyway. So don't feel bad about it. Oh, yes. There's a message on the phone from your mother. She says she won't be home until eight and you should go ahead and heat up the leftovers from last night and have your dinner." She looked at her watch. "So how about we go down to the kitchen and see what we can find. Okay? What kind of leftovers are we talking about? I'm hungry."

Of course Tree was just hanging around to be with Abby until Dorcas showed up, instead of starting the long drive home to her apartment in Berkeley. Which made Abby feel even more guilty about how she and Paige had ruined Tree's disguise and her chance to solve her first case.

But Tree didn't bring the subject up again. And a few minutes later the two of them were sitting in the breakfast nook, eating microwaved tamale pie and carrots and peas, and Abby was appreciating how Tree was finding other things to talk about besides what a mess she and Paige had made of everything.

They'd been over all the subjects people talk about when they're trying not to mention something in particular. Things like the weather, and how Abby was doing in her classes, and how many games the 49ers had won. It was Abby who finally brought up the subject they'd been avoiding.

"Well," she said, "other than having a couple of dumb kids blow your disguise, how was your day? Did you find anything out before we showed up?"

Tree's smile was, as usual, wide and uncomplicated, saying just what a smile was supposed to say, instead of slipping into a put-down as Dorcas's often did. "Nothing for sure," she said. "I went past the latest burn site a couple of times, and I did see some people hanging around. There wasn't much to see because the building was unoccupied when it caught fire. Most of the sightseers were staying outside the police tape, but a couple of guys in suits were poking around in what was left of the building. One of them was the owner of the building. I met him when he came to the office to ask Dorcas to take the case, and he would be hard to forget. He must weigh three hundred pounds and he has this huge hooked nose. I've never seen the other man before but he was probably the insurance company's arson investigator. The rest of them, the crowd outside the barrier, were probably just local rubberneckers."

"Or maybe the criminals returning to the scene of their crime," Abby said. "Aren't criminals supposed to do that? What did they look like?"

Tree thought a minute before she said, "Nothing you wouldn't expect. Most of them looked like curious neighbors. But then later some kids showed up—all ages. The older ones looked pretty tough. A lot like the ones who were getting ready to give you and Paige a bad time when I showed up. I wouldn't be surprised if some of them were involved in the arson. I described them all in my report. That's about all I was able to come up with. Except for an empty matchbook I found under a bush."

A sound echoed somewhere in the back of Abby's mind. A faint reverberation like the distant ringing of a gong. "A matchbook?" she asked.

"Yes. But there're very long odds against its having anything to do with the fire. Anyone could have thrown it down there. And I don't think it has the kind of surface that could carry much in the way of fingerprints."

Abby nodded. "Yeah, you're right," she said. "Anyone could have thrown it down." But the faint shiver of sound was still there, even when Dorcas called on her cell phone to say she had crossed the Bay Bridge and would be home in a few minutes, and it continued after Tree went to her car, calling back over her shoulder, "Just tell Dorcas my report is on her desk."

It wouldn't be long before Dorcas's Honda pulled into the driveway, but in that few minutes Abby could . . .

No. No. She couldn't and wouldn't.

Except that it had been at least partly her fault that Tree had lost her chance to solve the arsonist mystery and maybe be promoted to a real licensed private investigator. And Tree had always been such a good friend. A friend who, just tonight when she was probably tired and eager to get home, had stayed around just so Abby wouldn't be alone. So if there was any way to help Tree solve the mystery . . .

Abby was still shaking her head and arguing with herself as she went into the office, found the folder that held Tree's report, and took out several typed pages. At the back of the folder was an empty matchbook. Abby stared at the matchbook for several seconds before she reached out slowly and picked it up. She was holding it tightly in the palm of her right hand when it began to feel warm. Slowly at first, and then faster and stronger, everything began to spin.

As THE DIZZYING spin got stronger, the feeling of heat in Abby's palm became more distinct. It was a deepening warmth that soon began to leap and flare as if she were holding a handful of fire, a painless burning that surged up her arm, through her body, and into her brain. The rest of the Magic Nation craziness was there too, with spinning shreds and pieces coming together in a way that gradually blocked out the view of Dorcas's desk and the familiar office wall. And then suddenly everything went black. Complete and utter darkness—except for a tiny flicker of light.

The fire leapt up, died down, and grew again until its light began to illuminate the walls of a room—a dark, barren room where torn wallpaper dangled and where the paint on the walls and ledges was chipped and stained. The room seemed almost empty, except for the source of the mysterious flame. Flickering firelight was leaping from something shaped like a large bucket. The window curtains were flaming too, and the air was becoming heavy with smoke.

Then the pieces were breaking apart and spinning again, and the scene was changing. Now the light was cool and dim. Streetlights shining through heavy fog faintly illuminated an empty street where darkened windows gave a middle-of-the-night feeling. As the scene narrowed to the exterior of a large three-story apartment house, a man emerged from a doorway, looked carefully in every direction, hurried down the steps, and walked quickly away. As he approached the street, Abby could see him more clearly. Could see his huge bulky shape and his big shiny nose. He was wearing heavy gloves and carrying a large object in one hand. Just before he reached the sidewalk, he stopped long enough to throw something into a clump of bushes.

And then there was the familiar sound of a car in the driveway, followed by a click as Dorcas's key turned in the lock, and Abby came spinning back to the reality of the O'Malley Detective Agency office. Abby quickly put the matchbook back where she'd found it and slammed the folder shut, pushing it away from her across the desk. "No," she whispered. "No. I don't believe it. It doesn't mean anything." Turning away, she hurried to the kitchen in time to see her mother coming in the back door.

"Sorry to be so late." Dorcas took off her jacket as she looked around the kitchen. She was wearing her gray-green pantsuit and a turtleneck that Abby's dad had given her a long time ago, along with a bunch of jangly jewelry. "Have you eaten?" she asked.

"Yes," Abby said. "Tree helped me heat up some stuff and she ate some too. She stayed until you called. There's some of the tamale pie left. Are you hungry?"

Dorcas shook her head. "I ate at a deli while I was waiting to interview a woman who claims she could be a witness in the Anderson case. But I might have a cup of coffee."

While Dorcas made her coffee and took her cup to the breakfast nook table, Abby hung around drinking a glass of water and arguing with herself about what she should tell Dorcas and when she should do it. She knew all the facts would be in Tree's long, carefully written report. Including the facts about what she and Paige had done. All about how they had been stupid enough to go downtown without asking and had wound up blowing Tree's disguise. At last Abby took a deep breath and began. "I guess I have something to tell you, Mom."

"Yes? What is it then?" Dorcas looked up quickly and motioned for Abby to join her at the table. "Sit down. Tell me."

So Abby pulled out a chair and sat—and went on sitting while her mother's stare sharpened. "It's about a dumb thing that Paige and I did today." She paused, sighed, and went on. "It was Paige's idea but I went along with it, so it's my fault too."

"For heaven's sake, Abby. What happened? What did you do?"

"Well, my first mistake was telling Paige about the disguise I'd come up with for Tree, and Paige was . . . Well, you know how crazy she is about anything like that. She got so excited and she wanted to see if we could do something to help Tree catch the arsonist."

Abby told about how Paige kept them on the bus until they got nearly down to Van Ness. And about how the gang of boys had started after them and Tree had had to blow her disguise to come to their rescue. As Abby talked, Dorcas's eyes narrowed and her lips got tighter. It wasn't until Abby stopped that Dorcas started, but she had a lot to say.

When Dorcas was finished Abby's allowance was gone for two weeks, and Dorcas was going to call Daphne Borden in the morning, and after that, "Who knows? Daphne and I will have to come to a decision. Perhaps we'll have to arrange for you and Paige to see less of each other for a while. At least until both of you are able to behave in a more responsible manner."

Abby was shocked speechless. Not to see Paige? For how long? Dorcas hadn't said. Abby was fighting tears as she left the kitchen and went up to bed feeling so guilty, and at the same time so angry, that it was hard for her to think of anything else. Hard even to get back to what had happened, or had seemed to be happening, in the agency office when she'd picked up the matchbook. But once she started thinking about it, she couldn't stop.

What had she seen, really seen, when she'd held the matchbook in her hand? Where had the images come from and what did they mean? Wasn't it possible that she'd imagined a fat man with a big shiny nose simply because Tree had described such a person as the owner of the building?

It didn't make any sense. Why would anyone want to burn down his own apartment building? As she changed into her pajamas and got into bed, Abby went over all of it again and again. She went over exactly what she'd seen, or thought she'd seen, perhaps a dozen times while she tried and failed to go to sleep.

The questions she kept asking herself were what she had seen, and what did it mean, and hardest of all, what should she do about it? Should she go to Dorcas and tell her that she thought the man who owned the apartment building had set fire to it himself—and why she thought so?

And then . . . either it would turn out that she was right and Dorcas would say that her theory about Abby's supernatural abilities was absolutely true. Or else it would turn out that what she thought she'd seen was a bunch of nonsense, and that the owner of a building wouldn't be stupid enough to burn down his own property. And then Abby O'Malley wouldn't have to worry about being some kind of weird throwback to the days of witches and wizards. But what she *would* have to worry about was being even deeper in the doghouse than she already was, for making up a wild story to try to get herself and Paige out of trouble.

When morning finally came Abby was bleary-eyed from lack of sleep and still undecided about what she would do and who she would or wouldn't tell about the matchbook. But then fate, or just Dorcas's crazy schedule, took matters out of her hands, at least temporarily. Just as Abby reached the kitchen, the phone rang and Dorcas went to answer it, and a minute later she was throwing on her coat and rushing out of the house.

"There's oatmeal on the stove," she called to Abby over her shoulder. "And I haven't forgotten about talking to Daphne. It will just have to wait till I get back. Tree should be here in a few minutes. Tell her I had an urgent call from a possible witness."

Tree did arrive soon, in fact while Abby was still spooning up soupy oatmeal. (Dorcas's oatmeal was usually thick and lumpy except when she was in a hurry. Then it was apt to be more like oatmeal soup.) It wasn't particularly appetizing, but even so, when Abby invited Tree to have some, she said she would. Glancing at her watch, Tree said she thought there was time enough for a quick bowl of something nutritious, which she was really going to need because it looked as if she would be having another very busy day.

Abby sat across the table, watching Tree eat soupy oatmeal and being grateful that Tree hadn't even mentioned the mess Abby and Paige had made of her first surveillance assignment, when all at once she found herself saying, "Why would a person set fire to his own building?"

Tree looked up quickly and stared at Abby for a moment before she asked, "What person are you referring to, Abbykins?"

Even though Abby had more or less asked for it, Tree's question came as a shock. Now she'd have to come up with an answer that would get Tree thinking in a particular direction without admitting what she thought she knew and how she knew it. It wasn't going to be easy.

Abby shrugged. "Oh, I don't know. I was just wondering."

"But why? Why would you wonder about something like that?" Tree's eyes narrowed. "It wasn't one of those hunches your mother says you have, was it?"

"No. Not a hunch, at least not exactly. And anyway, why would a person burn their own building?"

Tree shrugged. "Well, it's been known to happen. Particularly if the building is in bad shape and the fire insurance is worth more than what the owner has invested in it."

"Oh yeah," Abby said excitedly. "I didn't think about that."

"Well, I sort of did." Tree's smile looked uncertain. "But Dorcas didn't really agree with me. She said this Mr. Barker seemed like such a law-abiding person. And she was impressed by the fact that he looked up our agency and asked us to investigate, even though the insurance company was already doing its own investigation."

"Yeah," Abby admitted reluctantly. "I guess he wouldn't have done that if he had anything to hide."

Tree shrugged again. She was grinning as she said, "Yes, that's what you might think, or else it might be what Mr. Barker *wanted* everyone to think. But you know what, Abbykins? I was there in the office when he came in to talk to Dorcas, and I got the feeling that maybe what he was really thinking was that an agency run by a couple of women wouldn't be much of a threat."

Tree glanced at her watch again and hurried off to open the office, leaving Abby to think over what had just been said. And the more she thought about it, the more convinced she became that Tree was right when she'd said this Barker guy had probably picked the O'Malley agency just because he was the kind of dude who didn't think women detectives could possibly be smart enough to mess up his plans. Particularly youngish women like Tree—and yeah, okay, like Dorcas too. Tree probably knew what she was talking about. After all, a person who looked like Tree Torrelli would have had a lot of experience in sorting out whether the men she met were telling her the truth about what they were thinking—or not.

So Abby went into the office, and when Tree looked up questioningly, Abby sighed and said, "Okay. So I guess I did have this kind of hunch about that fat Barker guy. Like, I had this feeling that he was the one who set the fire. Only I thought it was a dumb hunch because I didn't see why somebody would burn down his own building. But that was what the hunch was about."

Tree listened carefully, and when Abby stopped talking, she asked when Abby had had the hunch and what it had been like. But when Abby shook her head and said she'd rather not talk about it anymore, Tree didn't push it. However, she must have taken what Abby had said pretty seriously, because she closed up the office, went to the insurance company's office, and got them to get a search warrant to check out Mr. Barker's house and car, which they hadn't done before because Mr. Barker had an alibi—a friend who insisted they were together at the time the fire started.

Abby never found out exactly what Tree said to the insurance people, but that afternoon a fire-damaged bucket was found in the trunk of Barker's car, and the investigators also found at the back of his closet a pair of his shoes that had incriminating stuff on the soles. And when the police interviewed his friend again, the friend admitted that he'd been bribed to lie about being with Barker that night.

It turned out that the other two fires really had been accidents. One had been caused by a cigarette and the other by some bad wiring, but the two of them happening so close together probably gave Barker the idea that he could torch his own place and everyone would think it had just been one more attack by the neighborhood arsonist.

For the rest of that week, Abby was able to arrange her diary entries into two lists—a Bad News list and a Good News list. She put Mr. Barker's being arrested for arson under the Good News heading, but the fact that the O'Malley Agency didn't get, and never was going to get, all the money he'd agreed to pay them went under Bad News. On the other hand, the agency did get quite a bit more publicity, and that, according to Tree, was all to the Good.

Another good development was that although Dorcas did have the talk with Daphne she'd threatened, and both Abby and Paige did get seriously chewed out, that was about as bad as it got. For one reason or another, Dorcas seemed to have forgotten about insisting that Abby stop spending so much time with Paige.

The other Good News item was a very exciting e-mail that came on Friday from Abby's dad. The e-mail said that Mr. Montgomery, her dad's boss, had asked him how he would feel about moving back to his old office in San Francisco. That really was Good News in Abby's book. But from Dorcas's point of view? Abby wasn't too sure. When Abby asked her—came right out and asked her how she felt about it—Dorcas said, "I think it's great. Martin loves San Francisco."

But lots of people loved San Francisco, and there were all kinds of ways to say *great*. The way Dorcas said it was only great—not GREAT, and certainly not THE GREATEST.

9

SO THE ARSON case was solved by . . . well, by a hunch, but except for Abby and Tree, nobody knew whose hunch it had been. At first Tree had wanted to tell that it had been Abby who had fingered the arsonist, but Abby had begged her not to. They'd had quite a discussion about it the day after Mr. Barker was arrested. Dorcas had left early to follow her latest lead in a missing-person case, and Abby was passing through the office on her way to catch the bus to school.

"Oh good," Tree said when Abby came in. "I wanted to talk to you."

"Oh yeah?" Abby said. "What about?"

"About letting people know that you were the one who had the . . ." Tree paused and then went on. "The *hunch* about who the arsonist was." Her eyebrows went up when she said the word *hunch,* to show that she knew it had been something a little different from a good guess. Or maybe a lot different.

Abby quickly shook her head. "No. No. Don't. I don't want you to."

"Why not? You ought to get the credit for what happened," Tree said. "The insurance people are very grateful. They might even pay us some kind of bonus."

"But I don't want a bonus." Abby slid out of her backpack and sat down in one of the client chairs. "I don't want anybody to know that I had anything to do with it. And if you told the insurance people it was my *hunch* they'd be sure to tell other people, like . . ."

"Like?" Tree asked, but her smile said she could guess what the answer would be.

"Yeah," Abby admitted. "Like my mom."

Tree nodded. "Yes, I suppose they would mention it to Dorcas. But you know, Abbykins, what I don't understand is why you don't want your mother to know. I think she'd be delighted. I know she was when you came up with the idea that the Moorehead kid and her father might be at Disneyland."

Abby cringed. "I know," she said. She paused, looking at Tree thoughtfully for a moment. "Has my mom ever talked to you about how she thinks that I, well, both of us actually, can do weird things, like suddenly knowing things that we haven't any way of knowing, and stuff like that?"

Tree shook her head slowly as if she wasn't sure. "Well, not exactly," she said. "But she does talk about hunches quite a bit. She seems to have hunches quite often herself, but . . ."

"Go on," Abby said. "But what?"

Tree looked a little bit embarrassed. "I'm not saying your mom isn't a good investigator, because she is. She's hardworking and fantastically good at picking up on important details and remembering them, which is terribly important in our work. But as far as hunches go . . ." Tree shrugged. "Most of hers don't seem to help a lot."

"I know." Abby couldn't help sounding a little triumphant. "She's always telling me about the great hunches she's had, but most of them happened a long time ago. Like maybe she had good ones when she was a kid, but she's pretty much outgrown them now."

"But yours, on the other hand—" Tree began, and Abby hastily interrupted.

"Most of mine don't work either. Most of my hunches are no good at all."

"Well, another thing . . ." Tree looked uncomfortable. "When I went in to see Mr. Walters—he's the investigator at the insurance company—to urge him to get the search warrant, I told him I'd talked to someone who thought she'd seen Barker in the area on the night of the fire."

Abby grinned. "Which is the truth, in a way," she said. "Isn't that sort of what I told you?"

Tree looked even more embarrassed. "I know, but I implied that it had been some neighborhood woman. I don't know why, except I felt that getting the search warrant was urgent, like before Barker had a chance to get rid of the evidence. And I didn't think they'd take me very seriously if I said . . ."

"Yeah, if you said it was a kid who saw Barker. And especially if you said that the kid had seen him in a kind of . . ." Raising her eyebrows, Abby let her voice trail off.

"Vision?" Tree asked.

Abby shook her head hard. "No. Like I told you, it was just a guess." A disturbing idea occurred to her. "But what if the insurance people or the police want to talk to the person who saw Mr. Barker?"

Tree shook her head. "At this point I don't think they'll feel they need to. I told them the person who said she'd seen Barker didn't want to be identified." She grinned. "Which is true, right? And besides, when they found all that evidence in Barker's house and car, he more or less confessed. He admitted that he'd been there that night and might have set the fire accidentally."

"Some accident." Abby shrugged into her backpack. At the door she turned long enough to say, "Well, that's it then. It was *you* who figured out who the arsonist was. Nobody else. Okay?"

Tree grinned, sighed, and said okay.

So that was the end of the arson episode—except where Paige was concerned. Paige was absolutely hung up on the whole thing and how the case had been solved. And of course Paige, like everyone else—almost everyone else, that is—thought Tree had come up with all the clues that had solved the case. For a while it seemed to Abby that she and Paige were never going to talk about anything else besides the arson case—and Tree Torrelli.

The trouble was that Paige was the kind of person who always had to be absolutely fixated on somebody. A year or two before, it had been Leonardo DiCaprio, and right after that it had been Britney Spears. But now she seemed to have forgotten all about singers and movie stars and instead had become totally fascinated by Tree. She talked about her all the time, not only about what a great detective she was, but also, of course, about how totally gorgeous and glamorous she was.

At first Abby went along with Paige's Tree gush sessions, but before long they began to bother her. A lot. She wasn't sure just why, except that Tree had been her own private friend ever since she had begun working for Dorcas, and Abby had always known all the things about Tree that Paige was raving about. All the things except what a great detective she was, because she really wasn't, at least not right at first. But now, to hear Paige talk, a person would think Tree was a world-famous detective and Paige herself was the founding president of the Tree Torrelli Fan Club.

The picture thing was almost the last straw. Paige asked Abby if she had a picture of Tree, and when Abby admitted she did have an old snapshot, Paige insisted on seeing it. And then after she'd seen it, it somehow wound up on her bulletin board, right where she used to keep her favorite picture of Leonardo.

But it was even worse when Paige began to find reasons for visiting the office of the O'Malley Agency—and of course Tree. Like the time Paige started asking about the books Abby owned, and when Abby mentioned that she had three of the Lemony Snicket books, Paige insisted she had to borrow them, like immediately.

"Why?" Abby said. "I don't mind loaning them to you, but . . ." She grinned. "But I'll bet if you told your mother that you wanted to read the Lemony Snicket books, she'd buy you every one of them, like five minutes later."

"I know," Paige said. "But then I'd have to wait until they came in the mail, and I want to start reading them right now. So why don't we take your bus after school and I can just stop by your house and pick them up."

So Paige used her cell phone to call her mother from the bus stop to ask if she could go home with Abby, just long enough to borrow some books that she "really, really needed," and her mother said she would check with Abby's mother and call back. Then after about two minutes Paige's phone rang, and it was her mother calling to say that Abby's mother wasn't in but that she had talked to Ms. Torrelli in the agency office, and it would be all right for Paige to go by to pick up the books she needed. And then she was to wait right there until her mother picked her up on the way to take the boys to their karate lesson.

When they arrived at the O'Malley Agency, Paige spent about two minutes in Abby's room, where she grabbed the Lemony Snicket books, and rushed right down to the office to hang around staring at Tree and asking her questions in a nervous, gushy way, as if she were talking to some totally famous person. Watching Paige make a fool of herself over Tree really got to Abby. She went from feeling irritated, when Paige asked Tree how she'd learned to be such a great detective, to being really exasperated, when Paige started in on how Tree looked like a combination of Jennifer Lopez and the Olsen twins. At first Tree had just seemed amused, but Abby could tell she thought the Jennifer Lopez–Olsen twins stuff was pretty embarrassing.

By the time Abby finally got Paige out onto the front steps, where they were supposed to wait for her mother, Paige was raving that if she could look like anyone in the whole world, it wouldn't be Jennifer Lopez anymore; it would be Tree Torrelli. At that point something snapped, and Abby did an incredibly stupid thing. What she did was to say to Paige, "Well, if you want to know the truth, it wasn't Tree who figured out who the arsonist was. It was me. But I asked her to say she did it, and she said okay." Paige was staring at Abby in openmouthed amazement when the Bordens' Mercedes SUV pulled up.

"What? What do you mean?" Paige was asking when her mother honked, and she went down the steps, looking back at Abby with what was turning into a squinty-eyed, really suspicious stare. Abby stood on the front steps while the SUV pulled away with Paige glaring at her from one window and Sky waving enthusiastically from another. Abby waved back while her mind was busy elsewhere. Busy thinking, "Now you've done it, you idiot. Now you've really done it."

It wasn't long afterward, probably as long as it took Paige to get home, that the phone rang. "What do you mean you were the one who figured out who set the fire?" Paige demanded. When Abby insisted she couldn't talk about it on the phone, Paige kept saying, "Why not? I want to know right this minute." And then finally, "All right, then. Tomorrow morning. Okay?" And Abby had to agree.

ABBY LAY AWAKE for a long time that night asking herself how she could have been so stupid as to tell Paige that she was the one who had solved the arson case. Because now she would have to explain how it happened to be the truth.

Of course there was no logical, believable explanation. Not even one that Abby really believed herself. At least not for sure. After thinking it through about a million times, she finally decided that if there was any way to make Paige understand, it was to start at the beginning. As embarrassing as it would be, she was going to have to go into a lot of background stuff, such as Dorcas's crazy stories about Great-aunt Fianna and the other weird ancestors—and even more embarrassing, the whole Magic Nation thing.

Finally she turned on the light, and, getting out her notebook, she began to write down all the things she would have to tell Paige and the order in which she would do it. The list started out:

1. *According to my mom, her side of the family is descended from ancestors in Ireland or Wales who were some kind of psychic types. Especially one great-aunt named Fianna.*

2. *So the story goes, this Fianna person said that a lot of our ancestors could do stuff like read minds, and get messages about someone by holding one of the person's belongings in their hands.*

3. *The main reason my mom decided to become a detective was that she thought she could use some of the weird stuff she'd inherited to solve crimes. Only she's not very good at it. Not good at the weird stuff, that is. Actually she's a pretty good detective.*

4. *It looks like I might be the one who inherited some stuff. At least when I hold something that belongs to someone else in my hand, sometimes—not always, but once in a while—I can see a kind of vision about the person. That was how I found out about the arsonist.*

After she'd written and rewritten the list several times, she practiced reading it out loud. As she read, she tried to imagine what Paige's reaction might be to each thing on the list. Her first guess was that Paige wouldn't believe her and would just say something like "You're making that up, aren't you?" But then again—considering how crazy Paige was about all kinds of fantastic stuff—maybe not. After she'd thought some more, Abby began to guess that if Paige did get angry at her, the main reason might be because Abby hadn't told her before.

The next morning the conversation started just inside

the gate of the Barnett Academy the moment Abby got off the bus. Paige was right there waiting for her, and she hardly had both feet on the ground before Paige pounced like a cat on a mouse. Grabbing Abby by the straps of her backpack, Paige pulled her down the driveway as she whispered, "Okay. So tell me."

So Abby started the telling, and she hadn't gotten very far when she began to realize that nothing she'd imagined about Paige's reaction came even close. She'd rehearsed what to do and say if she met with a certain amount of suspicion, as well as how she might handle it if Paige got mad at her. What she hadn't prepared for at all was what she'd have to do and say if Paige believed every word of it and was totally thrilled to death.

Abby started, as she had decided would be necessary, by saying, "Well, according to my mom, we're descended from some ancient ancestors who were kind of like supernatural, and she thinks both of us inherited some things from them."

She got about that far before the last bell rang and Paige reluctantly turned loose of her backpack strap and let her head for her first-period class. The next time Paige caught up with her was during the lunch hour, when she once again appeared and dragged Abby away to an unoccupied table. That time Abby got into the whole thing about being able to hold someone else's possession in her hands to produce a kind of vision about the owner.

She could feel her cheeks getting red, and she found she couldn't look Paige in the eye as she went on. "I did it a lot when I was a little kid, and when I told the day care lady about it she said it was my imagination, only I thought she said it was my Magic Nation and for a long time I thought it was something that happened to everybody. That is, I did until my mom started telling me about us being descended from these weird ancestors."

Up until then Paige hadn't said anything, so Abby went on, still looking down at her hands. She told about how she had found the little Moorehead girl's locket on her mother's desk, and how it had made her have a kind of vision about Miranda and her father at Disneyland.

Paige, who had been amazingly quiet the whole time, finally broke in to say *"Wow!"* Abby looked up quickly, wondering, *Wow* what? Wow, what a liar, maybe?

Several seconds passed before Paige went on in a tense whisper, "That is so *insane!*"

Forgetting for a moment what *insane* meant when Paige said it, Abby said, "I know. I think so too. So please don't tell anybody. Promise you won't. Please?" It was then that she realized, mostly from the expression on Paige's face, that what Paige was saying was that she really believed what Abby had told her. Not only believed it, but was absolutely, *insanely* crazy about the whole idea.

"I knew it," Paige said. "That is, I should have known it. I should have seen that there was something totally supernatural about you."

"About me?" Abby winced. "Like what?"

"Oh, I don't know. Like the way you pick up things about what people are thinking and feeling. Like the way you knew about Sky's being caught in the refrigerator by Ludmilla. And the way you can do things without half trying."

Abby shook her head. "No, I can't. What kinds of things?"

76

"Oh, you know," Paige said. "Like the way you could ice-skate the first time you tried. And ski too. Like Ms. David said, that just wasn't natural."

Abby tried to interrupt to remind Paige that what Ms. David had said was that Abby was a natural, which meant something quite different, but Paige never stopped talking long enough for Abby to say anything.

That was about where things stood when the school day was over, except that, when Abby begged her to, Paige did promise she wouldn't tell anyone else. But by the time they were on the bus heading for Pacific Heights, Paige's enthusiasm had expanded to include some plans for the future. Plans about how she and Abby were going to form their own detective agency and start solving all kinds of mysteries by using Abby's psychic abilities. "We can call it the P. and A. Agency, for Paige and Abby," she said, "and people will hire us to solve all kinds of crimes and mysteries."

Paige's plan seemed to be for this "agency" to get under way immediately, even after Abby brought up a few difficulties they might run into. Difficulties such as being too young to get a detective's license, as well as the questions that were sure to come up when people brought them cases to be investigated and found out that neither one of them was quite thirteen. But Paige didn't seem to think that was going to be much of a problem.

"We'll just find our own cases to solve, then," she said. "I bet I can find some myself."

Abby was pretty skeptical, but it was only a couple of days later that Paige came up with a mysterious circumstance that she felt was a candidate for the honor of being the P. and A. Agency's first investigation.

The case involved an old woman named Mrs. McFarland, who had lived almost in the Bordens' backyard for a long time. The little house she lived in had once been the stable of the mansion next door to the Bordens'. The mysterious circumstance that Paige came up with was that Mrs. McFarland seemed to have disappeared. At least Paige hadn't seen her for quite a long time, several days in fact, and she felt quite sure that Mrs. McFarland had met with some kind of foul play.

"So," she said to Abby. "Why don't you just close your eyes and concentrate on Mrs. McFarland and see what you get?"

Abby tried to tell her that she didn't think it worked that way, but Paige went on insisting until she tried, closing her eyes and waiting to get some kind of a message about Mrs. McFarland. Nothing happened. No vision. Not even any uncomfortable feeling that something was terribly wrong, like she'd had when Sky had been about to die of fright from being captured by the cook.

"Don't you think she could be all right?" Abby said. "Maybe it's just that you didn't happen to be watching at the right time? I mean, couldn't she have gone in or out of the house when you were at school?"

"No way," Paige said. "I mean, every afternoon she walks down that little alley that I can see from the window of my own room. I see her there almost every day. And besides that, when she wasn't walking down the alley she was out in that garden you can see from the hall window. You know, pulling weeds and picking flowers and stuff like that. No. Something's happened to her. I'm positive. I'll bet if we got my dad's ladder out of the basement and climbed up and peeked in her window right now, we'd see . . ." Paige paused long enough to make her big round eyes get even bigger. "We'd see," she went on, "something totally horrible."

"Like what?" Abby swallowed hard. She was having mixed reactions. She couldn't help thinking that Paige's imagination was running away with her again. But imagining climbing up to peek in a window and seeing something really awful *was* enough to make the skin prickle on the back of her neck.

There was another scene that a much less active imagination could come up with quite easily: a scene that involved Paige and Abby too, way up on a ladder peeking in a window and being caught in the act by a perfectly healthy Mrs. McFarland, and probably a couple of policemen as well. A situation that, coming so soon after their going downtown without permission and messing up Tree's arson investigation, just might result in their parents deciding that they really shouldn't see much of each other for a while. Which would be totally unbearable, particularly since it might mean that Abby would have to give up going with the Bordens to Squaw Valley during winter vacation.

But when Abby came up with the suggestion that they just go down and knock on Mrs. McFarland's door and ask her if she was all right, Paige's response was not encouraging.

"As if," she said. "What if she's not dead?"

Abby thought that was a sensible question. "Well, okay. What if she isn't?"

"Well, that would really be scary," Paige said. "I mean, that woman really hates our whole family, especially

Woody and Sky. Actually, she hates everybody. That's one reason I'm positive somebody bumped her off."

Abby thought that was a good point, but she still had her doubts, and her lack of enthusiasm for the window-peeking expedition did manage to put the whole thing on hold, at least for the rest of that day. As it turned out, that was all it took. When Abby called Paige that evening about a math assignment, Paige answered her question and then said, "Oh, by the way, I guess Mrs. McFarland isn't dead after all. Woody and Sky were fooling around in her garden a little while ago, and she came out and whacked them with her cane."

Paige's sigh sounded disappointed. But after a moment she lowered her voice to a whisper and said, "But I'm on the track of something even *worse*. I'll tell you about it at school tomorrow." She hung up abruptly then, leaving Abby to wonder if what Paige was on the track of was worse than Mrs. McFarland being dead, or worse than her not being dead after all.

11

THE NEXT DAY Paige was waiting in the hall just outside their fourth-period class. The moment she saw Abby, she pulled her across the hall by the sleeve of her jacket and started whispering so fast that Abby couldn't make any sense of what she was hearing.

"Wait a minute." Abby was grinning as she finally managed to interrupt. "What are you raving about? What about a dead horse?"

Paige took a deep breath, looked around to be sure no one was within earshot, and started over. Speaking distinctly, she said, "Not a dead horse. A dead *corpse*. A body. There's a dead body out behind the goalpost."

Abby's smile froze. "A dead body! Where? What goalpost?"

"Right here. On our soccer field." Paige pointed toward the long strip of lawn that was used as the academy's sports arena. "See that big hedge between the goalposts and the fence? That's where. I noticed something kind of strange yesterday when I was chasing a ball that rolled back there. So right after the bell rang, I went back to investigate. And there's this big rectangle"—Paige made a shape with both arms—"where the ground is all loose like it was dug up not long ago. *And* there're some flowers scattered around on top of it. Petunias and irises, and like that."

Abby's breath came a little more normally. "Oh, I get it. You saw something that looks like a grave. But not an actual body."

Paige put her hands on her hips. "So, that makes it okay? I don't think so. Guess what gets put in a big grave. A big body. Right?"

"Like six feet long?" Abby asked. "Like a whole adult person?"

"Well, maybe not quite that long," Paige said. "But maybe long enough for a pretty big kid."

Abby nodded thoughtfully. "But it could be the body of an animal. I buried a blackbird once when our neighbor's cat killed it."

"What's that got to do with anything? You're talking about a little old bird. And you buried it in your own backyard, not on the school grounds. Do you think Mr. Cruz would let anyone on the grounds who was carrying a big dead animal? Not!"

Paige had a point. Mr. Cruz was the head custodian and he was always around in the mornings to check out the people who were arriving on the school grounds. "Well, how do *you* think it got there?" Abby asked. "Do you really think someone could climb over the fence carrying a big dead body?"

The fence around the school property was very high and sturdy. "Maybe not," Paige said. "At least a kid probably couldn't. But maybe an adult could. A big muscle-bound-type adult."

Abby moved down the hall to where she could see through the glass doors onto the playing field. Beyond the smooth green lawn, a really high fence was topped by a fringe of sharp pointed wires. "Well, it wouldn't be easy," she said. "But maybe a strong man with a tall ladder . . ."

The bell rang then and they had to hurry to get to Ms. Eldridge's fourth-period English class. But not to do much thinking about what the teacher was saying—at least Abby couldn't. Instead she sat with her eyes focused on Ms. Eldridge's face but with half of her mind out behind the soccer goal. When Ms. Eldridge asked everyone to write a sentence that contained a gerund, Abby wrote, *A murderer putting flowers on his victim's grave isn't too believable.* Fortunately she didn't get called on to read her sentence out loud, but later, when Paige saw it, she nodded and said, "I know. I thought of that. Except he might, if after he'd strangled her he looked at her beautiful face . . ." Paige acted it out, staring down tragically and then bringing her hands up slowly to cover what was obviously meant to be a guilty face. "In that case he might repent enough to put flowers on her grave, don't you think?"

Abby said, "Well, maybe." But it still didn't seem too likely.

Later that day, during her PE class, Abby got to inspect

the scene of the crime. While her team was warming up, she managed to kick a ball through the hedge and then run after it. Shielding her face with both hands, she pushed her way through a thick stand of prickly bushes until she looked up and there it was, just the way Paige had described it: a slightly mounded rectangle of freshly turned earth and, scattered over it, a few faded flowers. Clutching the soccer ball to her chest, Abby stared down at what definitely resembled a grave and for a moment let herself wonder if she could count on her ancestors, or whomever, to give her a clue as to who was buried there, and who had done the burying. Closing her eyes, she concentrated, but nothing happened. Not even the passing shadow of a hunch.

People had begun to wail, "Hey, Abby. Where are you? Where's the ball?" before she gave up and pushed her way back through the hedge. A little later, when she and Paige happened to cross paths briefly, she managed to whisper that she'd seen the grave.

"See!" Paige said. "What did I tell you? What are we going to do about it?"

"I don't know. I'll think about it," Abby said, and let the crowd move her down the hall.

"Okay," Paige yelled after her. "Meet me out in front right after school. Okay?"

On their way home on the bus that afternoon, and a little later in Paige's room, they talked in whispers about what they were going to do next. In whispers on the bus because two fifth-grade girls were sitting right in front of them, and in Paige's room because Sky had come in and refused to leave.

So Paige and Abby sat on Paige's ankle-deep throw rug and argued in whispers about whether they ought to tell the police, while Sky sat by the door and pretended to play a SpongeBob game on his Game Boy, but actually spent most of the time staring at Abby. The goofy googly-eyed staring thing was a behavior he'd developed right after Abby had saved him from being skinned alive. Abby didn't mind. Having an adoring six-year-old fan was a little bit embarrassing, but a definite improvement over having eggs dropped on her head.

At first Paige didn't want to tell the police. "I think we ought to solve it ourselves," she kept saying. "I mean, what could they do that you couldn't do better? All we—I mean, all *you* have to do is start using some of your supernatural powers."

"But I already tried," Abby said, "and nothing happened."

"Well, you didn't try hard enough," Paige said. Suddenly her eyes got that neon gleam, the way they always did when she was having an inspiration. It was a look that always made Abby feel excited, but at the same time, a little bit nervous. "I know," Paige was saying. "You need something to hold in your hand, like the Magic Nation thing. I'll bet that would do it. You need to go back out there to the grave and find something to pick up and hold, like . . ."

"Something to pick up?" Abby said sarcastically. "Like the dead person's arm? Or would just a finger be okay? No thanks, either way."

Paige shook her head. "No, not like that. At least not yet. But I think maybe if you got one of those flowers. One of those dead flowers. Whoever put it there must have held it in his hand for a while. So that ought to make it work. Right?"

Abby wasn't too enthusiastic but she finally agreed to try it as soon as she could get out to the grave site and get a flower. "But it probably won't be today," she said. "My gym class will be in the multipurpose room today. We're having badminton."

"All right, I'll do it," Paige said. "I'll get one of the flowers and slip it to you on the way home from school. Okay?" Giving Abby a squinty-eyed glance, Paige pantomimed sneaking something out from under her jacket and stealthily handing it over.

Abby sighed. She was reluctant to get involved for several reasons. If Paige got the flower to her without getting them both arrested on suspicion of something or other, and if the Magic Nation thing really worked, then what? If they really did solve a murder mystery, everyone would find out about it. First off they'd have to tell Dorcas, and then she would be sure she'd been right all along about Abby having inherited all that supernatural stuff. And the police would have to know and the newspapers and all the kids at school. And then the whole world would start thinking that Abby O'Malley, instead of being just a normal kid, was really some kind of weird supernatural monster. But if Abby tried and failed, Paige would probably think the whole Magic Nation thing had been a big lie from start to finish.

But reluctant or not, she knew that Paige would probably show up that afternoon with a flower, and sure enough, she did. The minute they were seated on the bus, Paige looked around carefully before she took a paper towel out of her backpack and unwrapped the faded, withered, and slightly muddy remains of a purple iris. "Here," she said. "I kicked the ball out through the hedge on purpose so I could go get this." She pressed the limp flower into Abby's hands. "Go for it." Then she sat there absolutely quivering with anticipation while Abby held the dead flower between her hands, closed her eyes, and waited.

It took a while. Nothing at all at first, but then the warmth began. It was only a faint echo of the warmth that had surrounded the pink locket, but a definite change in temperature. But when the spinning bits of light and shadow began to form a pattern, the results were much less clear. Mixed in among the flowing, flickering patterns of light, there did, at times, seem to be a face. Fleeting glimpses of a round-cheeked babyish face with wide tear-wet eyes were framed in what looked like a whole lot of stiff straw-colored hair. The face faded and came back and faded again. And then it was gone. Completely and irretrievably gone, and Paige was poking Abby and saying, "What is it? What did you see?"

Abby blinked and shook her head. "I'm not sure. It was sort of like a face, but I didn't see it very well."

"Whose face? Who'd it look like?"

"Not like anyone. I mean, not like anyone I know. But it mostly seemed to be a really young kid."

"A little kid." Paige sounded triumphant. "It must be the little dead kid who's buried out there. That's who it is, I'll bet."

Abby shrugged. "Well, maybe," she said, "but . . ."

The bus pulled to a stop and the conversation had to be postponed until later. A lot later, as it turned out, because Mrs. Borden was waiting to take Paige and the boys shopping for new ski boots. When Paige seemed reluctant, Mrs. Borden said, "It's now or never, dear. The season is already under way and you know your boots were already a bit too small last March. Jump in the car, girls. We can drop Abby off at her house." And then to Abby, "I just called and your mother is at home."

So that was as far as they got that day. Of course Paige called as soon as her shopping trip was over, but there were three phones at Abby's house and at least six at Paige's. And the dead body of a little kid wasn't the kind of thing you wanted to discuss when people might be listening in. People like Woody, for instance, whose favorite hobbies included listening to private phone calls.

That evening Abby went through the *Chronicle* looking for any stories about kids who had recently disappeared. Nothing there. And even though Abby and Paige were able to have a few short meetings at school, nothing was decided. Nothing except that they might have to tell somebody pretty soon. The question was, would it be Mrs. Greenwood, the principal, or Dorcas and Tree—or even the police? Paige had decided they ought to tell Tree first, but Abby didn't really want to tell anybody.

"At least not right away," she told Paige.

"But why not?" Paige demanded. "Why wait? The longer we wait, the less chance they have of catching the murderer. I mean, before he heads for the border or something. And if we tell the police, they might have pictures of all the little kids who are missing and one of them might be"—she rolled her eyes dramatically—"you know who."

Abby was reluctantly saying, "Well, I've been checking the papers and I didn't see anything," when the bell rang and the conversation ended before any decision had been reached.

That afternoon the rain, which had been threatening all day, finally started to come down hard, so when sixth period was over, the main hall was packed with kids trying to stay dry while they waited for their rides home. Abby was milling around in the crowd, waiting for Paige to show up before they headed for the bus stop and entertaining herself by looking at the kindergarten's bulletin board. Every class had a space in the main hall where they could post their artwork, and Abby had always liked to check out the kindergartners' work because it tended to be pretty original. Such as the self-portraits they'd done right after school started, when most of them were still drawing humans who were just one big circle filled with eyes, a nose, and a mouth, with stick-like arms and legs coming out of their heads.

She was noticing that now, a few months later, most of the people drawings had two circles, one for a face and a lower one to represent the body. She was grinning, thinking, Big improvement, when she almost fell over a very small girl who was staring at one of the portraits. Another one-circle effort but one where the face seemed to have long whiskers, and what looked at first like an extra pair of arms. Or else two very large ears.

"Oh, sorry. Did I step on you?" Abby asked.

The little girl shook her head, sniffed, and turned

around to stare up at Abby from under a bunch of stiff blondish hair. Wiping her eyes, she sniffed again and said, "You didn't hurt me."

"Then why are you crying?" Abby started to say when she suddenly realized exactly when and where she had seen that round-cheeked, tear-wet face before.

12

"BUT WHEN I asked her why she was crying," Abby told Paige, "she just shook her head and went, 'Because he's dead.' And when I went, 'Who's dead?' she kind of whispered, 'Bugsy. Bugsy's dead.' "

"Oh yeah?" Paige said. "I know about Bugsy. He's that big black rabbit they have in the kindergarten room. I guess he died, huh?"

Paige and Abby had reached Paige's room and were sitting in their favorite place on the fluffy rug. Back at school, when Paige had finally shown up and the two of them had pushed their way through the crowd to the bus stop, Abby didn't say anything at all. And when they were finally on the bus, breathless and a little bit damp from the rain, all she said was "I have something important to tell you."

"Well, tell me then," Paige had said, but Abby had

just shaken her head and rolled her eyes toward the two fifth-grade girls who, this time, had been sitting right behind them. "Wait till we get to your house," she said.

So they waited, but when they got to Paige's, they had another postponement while they dealt with Sky, who was waiting for them in the front hall. Running to stand in front of Abby, blocking her way, Sky said, "I have something for you."

"For me?" Abby said. "Okay. Where is it?"

Sky's hands were behind his back. "It's right here. Behind me," he said, but when Abby held out her hand, he giggled and jumped back out of reach. So she shrugged and started around him, only to have him jump in front of her again. That might have gone on for the rest of the afternoon if Paige hadn't snuck up behind Sky and snatched the wrinkled envelope out of his hands. Then she gave it to Abby while Sky jumped up and down shrieking and trying to get it back. When Abby opened the envelope and pulled out a piece of wide-lined paper, Sky wailed, "Oh no," and disappeared down the hall at a dead run.

Inside the envelope was a wrinkled piece of notebook paper covered with hearts and *X*s, and in big uppercase printing it was signed *Skyler Borden*.

"Well, what is it?" Paige asked, but when Abby said she thought it was a love letter, Paige snorted and said, "Holy cow." Then she grabbed Abby's arm and pulled her up the stairs.

It wasn't until they were safely hidden away in Paige's room that Abby finally got a chance to tell her about the little kindergarten kid who'd said she was crying because Bugsy was dead.

"Yeah, I remember Bugsy," Paige repeated.

Abby paused and then nodded slowly as she said, "And it wasn't until then, when the little kid started talking to me, that I realized where I'd seen her before."

"Where?" Paige asked, shaking her head and narrowing her eyes. "You mean like in the hall, maybe, or in the cafeteria?"

Abby sensed that Paige was about to guess but was trying not to. She was trying not to give up on her exciting theory that the face Abby had seen when she'd held the iris was the face of a murder victim.

Abby shook her head slowly and firmly. "No. Not in the hall. It was when we were on the bus and I was holding that iris in my hand. That was when I saw her face."

Frowning, Paige thought that over for a while before she said, "So why would you see *her* face? If the face you saw *wasn't* the murder victim's, why would you see it when you did the Magic Nation thing?" Paige gasped and her eyes widened. "Could she be the murderer?"

Abby couldn't help laughing. "A kindergarten murderer. No, I don't think so. I suppose she was just the person who held that particular flower, before she put it on the grave. So that's why I saw her. It was her flower."

"But why—who—what do you mean?" Paige was stammering when Abby interrupted.

"Just be quiet for a minute and I'll tell you. I'll tell you exactly what she said when I asked her why she was crying."

Screwing up her face into a sad-little-kid expression, Abby began, " 'Bugsy was our favorite pet animal and then he died. Ms. Wilton said he was a very old rabbit and he had a good long life and we shouldn't feel bad about it, but we did. And then Hillary said we should have a funeral. She said her family had one when their dog died and it made them all feel a lot better. So Ms. Wilton asked Mr. Cruz where we could have our funeral and he told us. So we did. And some of us brought flowers and Ms. Wilton got a great big box to put Bugsy in, and we all got to make pictures of Bugsy and put them in the box with him. Only I made an extra picture because I love Bugsy more than anybody. And then Mr. Cruz digged a great big grave. Only he told us not to . . . Oops. I forgot.'

"So I asked her, 'You forgot what?' And she said, 'Mr. Cruz told us not to tell other kids about the grave because he didn't want a lot of people tromping around through his bushes looking for it. So we promised we wouldn't.' Then she ducked her head and looked up at me from the tops of her eyes and said, 'But I forgot.' "

By the time Abby finished, Paige was glaring as if she thought it was Abby's fault their exciting murder mystery had turned out to be nothing but a bunch of kindergartners and their dead rabbit. But after a moment she shrugged and stopped frowning. "Okay," she said. "We'll just have to look for another mystery to solve. It won't take long. I found the first two in just a couple of days."

Paige thought for a minute, nodding slowly. "Maybe at Squaw," she said. "It won't be long until winter vacation. With all the lodges full of people maybe getting into fights on the ski runs, like those boys we saw last year who were trying to hit each other with their snowboards. Remember that? I'll bet we can find all kinds of crimes to investigate on the ski runs."

"Yeah, maybe," Abby said. But she was thinking, Or else we'll be too busy skiing.

After that nobody said much of anything for quite a long time. Abby stretched out on her stomach with her chin in her hands and thought about how soon it would be winter vacation and how much she was looking forward to it. And how lucky she was to have a friend like Paige, whose family owned one of the nicest cabins—if you could call a house with half a dozen bedrooms a cabin—in Squaw Valley and took Abby along with them three or four times a year just so Paige would have somebody her own age to ski with.

The scene she was imagining—or remembering— shifted from the view of the beautiful snow-covered forest that surrounded the Bordens' cabin to the valley floor spreading out far below the gondola. Picturing how the sleek silvery ski runs streaked down the mountain between thick patches of snowy forest, she couldn't help shivering in anticipation.

Then she was recalling, as she often did, the time Ms. David, the ski instructor, told the other beginners to watch Abby O'Malley because she was already doing a perfect snowplow. And of course, that other time, when she'd overheard Ms. David telling Mrs. Borden that she'd never worked with a beginner who was such a natural on the slopes. That had happened just four winter vacations before, the first year Abby had gone to Squaw with the Bordens. And Abby's plans to be an Olympic skier had started just about then.

Rolling onto her back, she put her arm across her eyes and let her daydream go from those remembered scenes at

Squaw to some imagined ones in which Abigail O'Malley was competing in a downhill or maybe a slalom. She imagined how she passed every gate smooth and tight, and how the waiting crowd cheered and waved when the loudspeaker called out her time. And then there she was, standing on the highest pedestal while they hung a gold medal around her neck.

But her dreams faded when Paige poked her and said, "Wake up. Did you hear me? I was saying that I really think we should look for at least one more mystery to work on before we go to Squaw. Don't you think so?"

So before she left for home, Abby had to agree to keep looking for suspicious events, which she did try to do now and then, between getting ready for midyear exams and doing Christmas shopping and decorating and all the other things that came before winter vacation. Occasionally she did take a few minutes to think about crimes and mysteries, but it didn't seem to be just now and then as far as Paige was concerned. It was pretty obvious that Paige's mind was still focused on finding another project for the P. and A. Agency to start working on. And wouldn't you know it, just as always when Paige set her mind on making something happen, before long she did seem to be finding some interesting possibilities. One of the first—in fact, you might say two of the first—concerned a certain hundred dollar bill that might, or might not, be a counterfeit.

The bill, which was a Christmas present Paige had received from one of her grandmothers, did have an unfamiliar look to it. The pictures of a grayish Benjamin Franklin on one side and the green-tinted building on the other might have been lighter shades of gray and green. And it certainly did feel a little different than most paper money. Which, of course, might be because Abby wasn't sure she'd ever seen a one-hundred-dollar bill before. At least not to hold in her own hands.

"See?" Paige said when she showed it to Abby on the bus one morning. "What did I tell you? It just doesn't look right."

Rubbing her fingers over the bill, Abby said, "Well, maybe. But perhaps it's just because it's very new."

But Paige was sure it was more than that. "I've had lots of new bills," she said. "Fifties and one hundreds. That grandmother always sends brand-new bills. But none of them ever looked as stiff as this one."

Abby was impressed. "Your grandmother always sends you fifties and one hundreds?" she asked.

Paige nodded absentmindedly. "Yeah, one of them does. The other one sends clothes. Things you couldn't pay me to wear. I like money better. Here!" Suddenly she held the bill out to Abby. "See what you can do with that."

For a moment Abby thought Paige meant that she should see what she could buy with one hundred dollars. It was an interesting thought, but when the money was pushed into her hand, and her fingers pushed down over it, she got the picture. Paige was suggesting that she should try the Magic Nation thing.

"Wait a minute," she said, feeling resentful and reluctant. Wishing, in fact, and not for the first time, that she had never, ever told Paige about the Magic Nation thing. "Even if it is counterfeit, what could I see that would prove anything? I think it only works when you're holding something that was close to the person it belonged to for quite a while. The longer, the better. And this bill doesn't look like it ever was in someone's pocket, and not even in a wallet. At least not for very long."

"Well, try it anyway," Paige said. "Maybe you'll see a building where they're printing counterfeit money and their name will be on the building or something."

"Whose name?"

Paige sighed and looked exasperated as she said, "Whoever printed the bill and passed it off on my poor dumb grandmother. Go on. You can try, at least."

Even though she thought the whole thing was pretty useless, Abby closed her fingers over the bill, closed her eyes, and waited—and waited some more. After a while the warmth started, but not much. Not even enough to be sure it was really happening. And then what seemed to be a vague, distant form of the bits and pieces started whirling through the air. The pieces came together and bounced apart, never staying long enough to form a real picture, except after a while one that looked a little like Paige herself. A Paige who was leaning forward and staring, just as she was really doing when Abby opened her eyes.

"All right," Paige was demanding. "What did you see?"

Abby grinned. "I saw you," she said.

Paige looked startled, but then she smiled and nodded. "Sure," she said. "Because I was the last one to hold it. But you didn't see who had it first, or who made it?"

Abby shook her head. "Nothing else."

Paige frowned. Giving Abby a look that said she was a big failure, Paige grabbed the hundred dollar bill and stuffed it angrily into her wallet. Then she turned her back and didn't say anything else until the bus stopped, and went on not saying anything while they got off and walked side by side to the school entrance. Abby didn't see her again until lunchtime.

Abby was still arranging the different parts of her lunch neatly on one of the lunchroom tables, as she always did before she started to eat, when she looked up and saw Paige approaching. She was bracing herself for some more of the silent treatment when Paige plopped down beside her and said, "Okay. Wait till I tell you what kind of crimes are going on right here at the academy. Right here in Mrs. Patterson's art class."

Feeling relieved, Abby said, "So tell me. What's going on?"

"Well, there are thieves in the class. One, anyway, and probably some other kids were in on it."

"Oh yeah? What are they stealing?"

Paige's eyes narrowed. "My hundred dollar bill, for one thing. The one I showed you?"

"Yeah?" Abby was shocked. "You mean someone stole your money?"

"That's what I'm trying to tell you. When I went into the class this morning, I put my pack down and was getting my stuff out when Alix and Megan started fooling around at the back of the room, doing a kind of karaoke routine, and everybody went over to watch. I did too. *And,* while I was gone and everyone was watching the dumb stuff Alix and Megan were doing, somebody opened my pack and took my hundred dollars."

"Out of your wallet?" Abby asked.

Paige nodded slowly and significantly. "Yes. *You* saw me putting it there this morning. You could be a witness about how you saw me put it back in my wallet when we were still on the bus. Right?"

"Yes. You did put it in your wallet. And you're sure you didn't take it out again after that?"

"Yes. Why would I take it out? After that I was just in class."

After a moment Abby grinned. "Well, it would serve the thief right if it does turn out to be counterfeit, wouldn't it?"

A grin replaced Paige's frown. "Hey. You're right. I hadn't thought of that. I sure hope it is." But then the frown returned. "So. What are we going to do about it?"

Abby didn't have an answer. During the rest of the day she now and then thought about the two mysteries concerning Paige's money. Counterfeit or not? Stolen or not? Paige had said, "What are *we* going to do about it?" But the way she'd looked at Abby when she'd said it made it clear that what she meant was "What are *you* going to do about it?" As if she were counting on Abby to do some kind of a Magic Nation stunt and solve everything.

And once again Abby wished she had never told Paige about Great-aunt Fianna and the supernatural ancestors stuff. Paige seemed to think that Abby could, if she wanted to, do an abracadabra and get all the answers, which made Abby feel like some kind of weird fortune-teller type. Like maybe she ought to go around wearing fringed shawls and carrying a crystal ball. The whole idea was ridiculous. What could she do? There was nothing to hold in her hand. And as for any other psychic stuff, such as reading minds or predicting things, she knew those weren't things you could just choose to do. They happened to you or they didn't, and you never knew when they would happen, or how or why. What she wanted to tell Paige was that she couldn't do any of it anymore—if she ever had been able to. Maybe the whole thing had just been her imagination, like Mrs. Watson said.

She really had tried to think about the money and picture the place it came from, as well as where it might be at the moment. But nothing was there. The only thing that kept coming to mind when she thought about the hundred dollar bill was how angry Paige had looked when she was stuffing the money back into her wallet.

That night Abby was starting to write in her diary about how Paige seemed to be sure she could find the hundred dollar bill if she wanted to when the phone rang and Dorcas yelled up the stairs to say the call was for Abby. So Abby went down to the kitchen to take the call, and of course it was Paige.

"Hi," Paige said. "Can you talk?" which was code for "Is anybody listening?"

And since Dorcas was sitting right there in the kitchen, reading the paper and finishing her coffee, Abby had to say, "No, I can't."

"Neither can I," Paige said. "I'm sure somebody is listening in."

Then Sky's voice said, "Yeah, you're right. Woody is, on the phone in the hall."

Paige and Abby laughed, and Abby said, "And where are you listening in, Skyler Borden?"

"I'm in the library," Sky said. "And I'm not listening in. I'm just telling on Woody."

Paige and Abby laughed some more, and then Paige said, "Well, I'm just calling to tell Abby that I have something important to tell her. I have something important to tell her tomorrow on the bus. Got that, Woody?"

13

THE NEXT MORNING, as soon as she got on the bus, Paige announced, "My bad. My money wasn't stolen after all."

"Hey," Abby said. "Did you find it?"

Paige looked sheepish. "It was right there in my wallet, wadded up in the coin purse part. I never put paper money in there, but I must have done it while my mind was on something else."

Abby grinned. "Your mind was on being mad at me for not being able to find out who the counterfeiters were, I guess."

"Yeah. Well, maybe." Paige nodded, ready as usual to admit she'd been the one in the wrong. "And besides, I've changed my mind about it being counterfeit. After it got wadded up in the coin purse it started looking pretty normal."

So with only a few days left before winter vacation, both of the hundred-dollar-bill mysteries had fizzled out, nothing else had come up, and Abby thought that with any luck she could start concentrating on getting ready for Squaw. But it wasn't going to be quite that easy.

Paige's next idea was that although she and Abby hadn't been too successful at discovering crimes that needed to be solved, it didn't necessarily mean they wouldn't be good at solving one that somebody else was already investigating. Somebody like Dorcas, for instance, or maybe . . . Tree.

When Paige started asking all sorts of questions about what the O'Malley Agency was working on at the moment, Abby shrugged and said, "Nothing that I know about. Dorcas doesn't tell me about her cases. At least not any of the important ones."

"Oh yeah? Then how'd you find out about the Moorehead case, and that arson thing?"

"Just by overhearing my mom talking to people, I guess, mostly on the phone. I don't listen on purpose. It just happens sometimes."

"Well, what have you overheard lately?"

Abby shook her head, but because Paige looked so disappointed, she thought some more and said, "Oh yeah. I guess Tree has this one dumb case about some next-door neighbors suing each other because one family's dog bit the other one's kid. I heard my mom talking to Tree about it. It's been going on a long time but neither side will give up."

"Oh!" Paige's face lit up. "What is Tree doing on the case?"

Wishing she hadn't mentioned Tree, Abby said, "Well,

the family with the dog say the boy kicked it first, so they hired the agency to find out if the kid has a record of mistreating animals. So I guess all Tree is going to do is check at the kid's school and with other people in the neighborhood."

"Oh," Paige said again, nodding slowly for a moment before her eyes started doing their neon glitter. "Hey. I know. Maybe we could go to the kid's school and ask the other students if the guy has been mean to any of their pets."

Abby sighed deeply. "Look," she said. "After what we did to Tree's investigation of the arson thing, what I think is, if she found out we were planning to help her again she'd probably leave town."

Paige stared at Abby for a moment before she shrugged. "Yeah. Guess you're right." But then the lights came on again. "Maybe we could keep it a secret. That we were helping, that is. At least until we'd found some important clues that would really help her win her case, and then we could . . ."

It was then that Abby surprised herself by putting her foot down, something she almost never did where Paige was concerned. At least not very successfully. "No," she said. "No. I'm not going to." Something, maybe her tone of voice, must have convinced Paige to stop making plans to get involved. Or perhaps just to stop telling Abby about it.

In the meantime Christmas approached, and for a while the Bordens were busy with a bunch of their relatives from the East Coast. And the O'Malleys were busy too, buying and wrapping presents and planning for a dinner that would be for just the two of them, since Tree was having Christmas with her big Italian family. But then there was a real change. Abby's dad called on Christmas Day to say he was back in town, staying in a hotel while he looked for an apartment to rent—*and* Dorcas asked him to come to Christmas dinner.

Abby tried not to be thrilled and excited, but she was, even though she kept reminding herself that it probably didn't mean anything. Not anything for certain anyway. One minute she'd find herself thinking, Maybe it does, and the next minute, Maybe not. Up and then down. Down and then up. It took another carefully written Good News, Bad News entry in her notebook to slow the teeter-totter down.

Under Good News she wrote:

1. *It happened. Dad really did get transferred back to San Francisco.*

2. *We'll probably get to see him a lot more often. At least I will.*

3. *He's going to be here for Christmas dinner.*

But under Bad News she reminded herself of all the times her dad had visited before that hadn't changed anything. One more thing she did was look up some new recipes of the quick-'n'-easy type and see to it that Dorcas followed them carefully on Christmas morning.

That night at the dinner table, the conversation started out about San Francisco and what a wonderful city it was. "Absolutely the greatest," her dad said, and *then* added, "I can't wait to get back home."

Abby looked up quickly, wondering if "back home" just meant back to the city where he grew up—or maybe something more. But when she caught his eye, he only did his lopsided pirate's grin and shrugged in an offhand way. A moment later he did it again at Dorcas and she smiled back.

When they were through eating, Abby's dad said a lot of complimentary things about the food, and then he and Dorcas started teasing each other about some awful cooking disasters they'd had when they were first married. Like the time they'd tried to make a spaghetti dinner for a bunch of friends by pouring some canned sauce over raw spaghetti and putting it in the microwave. "Well, I didn't lie to you." Dorcas was still laughing. "I told you I couldn't cook. And I also remember that you promised we'd watch some cooking programs on TV and learn how together."

Abby's dad grinned again and said, "Guilty as charged. Dropped the ball on that one too, didn't I?"

Abby was intrigued. But then, just as she was sure she was going to learn some important family secrets, they switched over to talking about boring stuff like politics, which was one thing they absolutely agreed on.

But on the whole the evening went pretty well; at least there weren't any of the usual arguments. Not even the one about how Dorcas could do just as well financially and have a lot less stress if she'd sell the agency and go back to being a legal secretary. That was an argument that Abby had always had mixed feelings about. She could understand why Dorcas wanted to prove she could be a success in a career she had chosen for herself. One at which she had been doing pretty well, at least recently. But Abby's dad's argument that there were careers that would leave her more time for other things—and other people—was probably true too.

After dinner they opened their presents. Abby got a lot of great stuff, including some new goggles and mittens from Tree and a great Obermeyer ski outfit from her mom. And from her dad, a digital camera no bigger than a wallet. So it was a good Christmas, even though how Dorcas and Abby's dad felt about each other didn't seem to have changed all that much. Not for sure, anyway.

Then school started again, and almost immediately Abby began to feel that Paige was still up to something. Part of it was just a vague feeling that Abby couldn't quite put her finger on, but the other part was that Paige had again started insisting on visiting Abby instead of the other way around. One time it was because she wanted to go through Abby's bookshelves again to see if there was anything else she wanted to borrow, but as usual she spent most of the time in the office just watching Dorcas and Tree while she only pretended to be reading one of Abby's books. And then the very next day, when the only person in the office was a woman from the steno pool, Paige showed up again.

That time she did stay in Abby's room for a while, talking about favorite books and authors, but then she went down to the kitchen to get a drink of water. At least she said that was where she was going, but when she didn't come back, Abby found her in the agency office. The steno had gone home, and there Paige was, going through the cabinet in which Tree kept files of the cases she'd been working on. When Abby opened the door, Paige jumped, pushed the file cabinet shut, and gave Abby a guilty smile.

"Okay," Abby said. "What are you doing?"

"Oh, I was just . . . I was . . . I . . ." Paige stuttered nervously for a minute before she suddenly stuck out her chin and said, "All right. I was looking for Tree's file on that biting dog–kicking kid case. All I wanted to do was find out where those people lived, and then I was going to call a cab so we could go there and find something you could use to do your Magic Nation thing on. You know, something like a ball that belonged to the kid, or one of the dog's bones."

"Look, Paige," Abby said, "besides being pretty sneaky, you're not making much sense. The Magic Nation thing wouldn't help. What it might do, if it does anything, is show me what the person who owns the ball, or bone or whatever, is doing right now, or at least not very long ago. Not what he might have done several months ago, or whenever it was that he got bitten. I heard Mom tell Tree that this case had been going back and forth for ages."

But Paige didn't give up. "What's wrong with seeing what he's doing right now?" she asked. "Who knows? If we find something that belongs to the kid maybe you'll see him kicking someone else's dog. That would prove he's probably guilty, wouldn't it?"

"Holy cow," Abby said. She could just picture herself and Paige being caught snooping around in some strangers' backyard looking for who knows what. "I think I'm getting a Magic Nation picture right now," she told Paige. "A picture of both of us in the back of a police car on our way to juvenile hall."

Paige stared wide-eyed, but then she grinned and shrugged. "Yeah, I guess you're right. My bad. Let's talk about something else. Like getting ready for Squaw. I've been meaning to ask you if you'd like to have my last year's ski boots. They don't fit me anymore, but I think they'd be just the right size for you."

Abby remembered the great Lange boots, which, when the season ended, had still looked as good as new. So she grinned and said thanks and forgot about being mad, and they started talking about skiing and about maybe starting to snowboard, something they might do if Paige could get her dad to change his mind about wanting them to become expert skiers first because that was the way he'd done it.

"That's my dad for you," Paige said. "My way or no way. Don't you wish he'd let us start snowboarding right away?"

"Yeah, I guess so," Abby said, "but I still think skiing's a lot of fun."

"Well, sure," Paige said, "but I think snowboarding would be a lot more exciting. I mean . . ." She paused, waggling her eyebrows. "Remember those snowboarders who kept scaring people off the runs last year?"

"Yeah, I remember." Abby was puzzled. "So is that why you want to snowboard? You want to scare people off the runs?"

Paige shrugged. "No. Of course not. I'd just like to meet some of the guys who do it." She waggled her eyebrows again. "Know what I mean?"

Abby knew what Paige meant. The year before, a lot of the snowboarders seemed to be teenage boys. The kind of teenage boys Paige called hunks, which of course meant good-looking—but when Paige said it, it seemed to have something to do with the way they acted too. The way they went around being totally cool. Too cool to notice things such as where they were going or who might be in the way. Abby grinned. "Yeah," she said. "I know what you mean."

The last day of school finally came and went, and on a bright sunny Saturday morning, the Bordens' newest SUV pulled in front of the agency, and Mr. Borden got out to help Abby add her skis to the five pairs that were already on the roof. Abby hugged Dorcas and Tree good-bye and climbed into one of the mid-row seats. Dorcas and Tree were waving from the front steps of the agency, and everyone inside the SUV was waving back, except maybe Woody, who was pretending to be too busy with his Game Boy to notice. The SUV pulled away from the curb, heading for the Bay Bridge and, before the day was over, Squaw Valley.

14

THE TRIP FROM San Francisco to Squaw Valley only took a few hours, but they were hours that always seemed to crawl by because it was just so hard to wait for the days out on the slopes, schussing straight down favorite runs so fast it was almost like flying, and doing bigger jumps and smoother slaloms every day. And for the nights in an attic room way at the top of the Bordens' cabin, where Abby and Paige would look out into the snowy forest and talk and laugh while the rest of the house grew dark and silent. So, as always was the case when you were waiting for something wonderful to happen, the hours really dragged. Daydreaming helped to pass the time, along with keeping her notebook handy so that she could follow their progress on a map of California.

On this trip the long hours in the car seemed to bother Paige even more than they did Abby; at least she certainly griped about them more. Along with minor complaints about things such as not being allowed to choose where they would stop for lunch, her biggest gripe on this trip was about the way the seats were arranged in the new SUV. In her opinion Woody and Sky's backseat was way too close to the ones she and Abby sat in. This meant that it was impossible for Abby and Paige to talk about anything private without being overheard, and that they were forced to overhear every word of the frequent arguments about which one of Paige's brothers had trespassed one fingertip into the other one's private space. In addition to the arguments about trespassing, there was a lot of other stuff Abby and Paige had to try not to hear. Stuff such as Woody's constant telling and retelling of favorite little-boy dirty jokes, most of which were about things like barfing or going to the bathroom.

That year's trip was turning out to be a little better than others in some respects. Particularly in the way Sky had stopped helping with any attack against Abby and even tried to come to her rescue in some situations. For instance the time he whispered, "It's okay. It's only a rubber one," just before a huge black spider appeared on her shoulder. It was a warning that didn't register quite soon enough to keep her from almost jumping out of her skin. And another time, when they stopped to have chains put on the tires and everyone got out in the snow to stretch. As they were getting back into the car, Sky whispered, "Keep your hood up," another warning Abby didn't really understand until Woody put a handful of snow down Paige's sweater.

The hours did pass, however, the snow beside the road got deeper and whiter, and the SUV finally turned up the driveway that led to the Bordens' cabin. Then all the good memories came flooding back, making rubber spiders and dirty jokes seem unimportant. Good memories of the unbelievable beauty of snowy hillsides, and of the thrill of discovering that she, who had never even seen snow until she was eight years old, was a "natural" who had been "born to ski."

Abby thought the Bordens' cabin at Squaw was fantastic, even though she could guess what Dorcas might say about it. She could imagine comments about how somebody had worked awfully hard, and spent tons of money, to make the whole thing look kind of old and handmade, with its fireplaces built out of rough stones, and ceilings supported by tree trunks still covered by bark. But none of that had anything to do with why Abby always felt so great when they finally pulled up the long driveway and she and Paige jumped out and began to move all their stuff into their private room up at the top of the house.

That night all the Bordens and Abby had dinner at Plump Jack's in a dining room crowded with dozens of other skiers and snowboarders of all ages. Including, at the next table, a couple of teenage boys. Actually Abby was sitting with her back to the boys' table, and she might not even have noticed them if Paige hadn't kept poking her and, with wildly waggling eyebrows, pointing over Abby's shoulder. Abby's first thought was that Woody's spider had reappeared, but she finally got the message and managed to turn around and take a quick look.

"Did you see them?" Paige's eyes certainly had their super-focused gleam.

"Yeah, I guess so," Abby whispered back. "Who are they?"

"You mean you don't recognize them?" Paige was amazed. "They're the ones I was talking about. The snowboarders, from last year. You know, the ones who—"

Just then Paige's mother asked what all the whispering was about, and Paige made her eyes go round and blank as she said, "Whispering? We weren't whispering. Were we, Abby?" While Abby was trying to decide whether to nod or shake her head, Paige was going on. "What do you want us to do, Mom? Shout? You want us to shout at each other?"

The people at the next table, including the two interesting snowboarders, left just before the Bordens did, and Paige poked Abby even harder to be sure she didn't miss getting a better look at them as they went out. But even then Abby didn't get to see them very well. Just well enough to notice that the taller one had blond hair and the other guy had so much dark hair that it curled down over his ears. Both of them were fairly tall and probably pretty old. Maybe fifteen, or even sixteen. She might have seen them better, except that just as Abby was turning to look, Paige suddenly fell out of her chair.

"Oh, sorry," Paige said, getting to her feet. "I dropped my napkin."

It wasn't until later, when they were all back in the cabin and Paige and Abby were finally alone in their room, that Abby found out what really had been going on. In their bedroom at the top of the house, with its wide padded seat that ran all along one wall under windows that looked out into deepest forest, they turned off the lights, wrapped themselves in blankets, and talked for hours, just as they had so many times before.

They talked first about how all the waiters and busboys

at the restaurant had said their winter vacation had come at just the right time because the snow was perfect, deep and fresh and neither too wet nor too dry. Just thinking about all that beautiful new snow caught Abby up in wonderful memories of thrilling downhill runs. She could hardly wait for it to begin. Shivering excitedly, she asked, "So where will we start tomorrow? Which lift should we take first?"

And Paige's answer was "Well, that's something I want to talk to you about."

Abby was pleased. Usually Paige was the one who made decisions such as that. Abby began, "Okay. After we leave the boys off at the Children's Center I guess we might as well start with the Belmont just to get warmed up, and then in the afternoon—"

Paige interrupted. "Yeah, you're right about having to leave the boys off. Dad and Mom will want to get an early start so they can get to KT before it crowds up. But as soon as we get rid of the brats I know what we should do." The way Paige's eyebrows were behaving was beginning to give Abby an idea, or at least the beginning of an idea, of what was coming. Sure enough, what Paige said next was "I think we ought to go to whatever run those snowboard guys are going to be on. You know, the ones whose table was right near ours."

"Well, okay." Abby couldn't help grinning. "But how are we going to know . . ." But before she could finish the sentence, she began to get a premonition about what the answer was going to be.

Sure enough, she'd hardly started her question when Paige answered it. "Here, I'll show you how." She jumped off the window seat and ran to the closet, dug into her jacket pocket, and came back carrying a big white piece of cloth by the tips of her fingers. "Here," she said, pushing it into Abby's hands. "What do you think that is?"

"Looks like a napkin," Abby said.

"Yeah. You got it. A napkin from Plump Jack's." Paige looked triumphant.

Having been brought up by a mother who was so much into law and order, Abby couldn't help feeling a little shocked. "You stole a napkin from Plump Jack's?"

Paige shrugged. "No, I didn't. I just borrowed it. I'll take it back when you're through with it."

Now Abby was pretty sure she knew what was coming next. Not the whole thing, maybe, but at least a general idea. It was an uneasy feeling.

Paige went on to say, "One of those snowboarders used this napkin. The blond one. You remember when I said I dropped my napkin last night? Well, what actually happened was that I noticed that he dropped his napkin when he got up to leave, so I dropped mine and when I went to pick it up I kind of fell out of my seat so I could reach across and pick up his. Get it?"

"Yeah," Abby said. "I get it. But what I don't get is what *I'm* going to do with it."

Paige sighed impatiently. "You don't? Well, didn't you say that when you do your Magic Nation thing, you usually see where"—Paige paused dramatically and then went on—"*where* the person the object belonged to is right at that moment? Like, how about, which run the person happens to be snowboarding on."

For a long moment Abby stared at Paige, and Paige stared back, making her face say a series of things, starting with "Isn't that a great idea?" and then after a while, "Well, what's wrong with it?" At last she growled, "Why not?"

"Well, for one thing I don't think it will work. Like I told you, it doesn't always, especially if I'm, like, expecting it to."

Paige looked suspicious. "I don't get it. Why wouldn't it work when you're expecting it to?"

"I don't know. I can't explain it. But it's not something I can turn on like the Weather Channel to see if it's going to rain. It's just something that happens sometimes when it's . . ." She faltered to a stop and then went on, "I guess when it's *important* enough."

Paige put her hands on her hips and said sarcastically, "And, like, who gets to decide whether it's important or not?"

"I don't know," Abby said. "But I know it's not me."

As Paige got off the window seat and headed for her bed, she turned back long enough to say, "Well, I guess we'll find out what's really important tomorrow. Okay?"

15

FINALLY CUDDLED INTO her built-in bunk bed in a cozy nest of blankets and comforters, Abby had trouble going to sleep. She didn't know why. She told herself it was probably just excitement about where she was and what would be happening the next day. But after a while she knew there was more to it than that. Part of it was made up of stuff she'd worried about before when Paige wanted her to do the Magic Nation thing. Stuff such as, what would happen if the napkin didn't bring up anything at all?

Or what if it worked in a way that didn't make clear just what she was seeing? After all, there were more than thirty lifts in Squaw Valley. What if she just saw Paige's snowboard hunks going down a run somewhere? Somewhere, but where? For instance, when she'd seen Miranda at Disneyland, she wouldn't have known where Miranda was if she hadn't been so familiar with the place. It wasn't as if there'd been a big finger pointing to a DISNEYLAND sign. And she didn't remember seeing signs along the ski runs either. No big road signs saying YOU ARE NOW HALFWAY DOWN SQUAW ONE EXPRESS or RED DOG.

When she finally sank into a restless sleep, she had a long scary nightmare in which she was trying to catch up with a lot of people on snowboards who, just as she almost got to them, kept taking off and flying through the air like remote-controlled model planes. And then she was the one holding the remote, and people were yelling at her to keep the flying snowboards from crashing into each other. Daylight came at last and Paige was shaking her, saying, "Hey. Wake up."

Breakfast at the cabin had always been fun, if rather hectic. It was what Paige's dad called Every Man for Himself. That meant you had to pick something out of the freezer or refrigerator and zap or toast or boil it all by yourself. It seemed to be a favorite time of the day for all the Bordens, which was probably because it was such a novelty. At home nobody fooled around much in Ludmilla's kitchen, not even Paige's mom.

Watching little old Sky get a carton of orange juice out of the refrigerator and pour it very carefully into a glass reminded Abby of how she'd rescued him from being "zkinned alive," and it must have reminded Sky too, because when he noticed Abby watching him, he went into a blushing, blinking, squirming fit. And then, staring at Abby adoringly, he went on pouring until his glass filled up and slopped over. While she was helping him mop up the large orange juice puddle, Woody started teasing.

"Roses are red, violets are blue, Sky's got a girlfriend,

and I know who," Woody was chanting when Sky threw a sponge at him. Of course Woody threw it back, and no telling what might have happened next if Mr. Borden hadn't walked into the room.

As soon as a certain amount of eating was accomplished, there was what Mr. Borden called an Area Beautification Project, which meant that everyone had five minutes to clean up whatever mess they'd made, before they all got into their jackets and helmets and ran out to the SUV. Halfway down the drive they had to stop and back up so that Woody could go back for his gloves, but then, at last, they were off.

As the SUV slipped and slid over the snowy road that led to the village, Abby was, as always on the first day of skiing, quivering with excitement. Except that this time some of the quivering might have been caused by a feeling that was more like nervousness. Nervousness about what was going to happen as soon as they were out of the car and on their own.

While they had been getting dressed that morning, and later in the kitchen, Paige hadn't mentioned the words *napkin* or *Magic Nation,* and she went on not mentioning them as she and Abby were getting out of the car, telling Daphne and Sher to have a great day, and escorting Woody and Sky to the Children's Center.

At the center, while they waited for the boys' instructor to arrive, Paige went on chattering about her new boots and what kind of helmets she hated because they made you look like a big-headed alien. However, Abby had a distinct feeling there was something else behind all the chatter just waiting for the right moment. But the moment hadn't arrived before the instructor showed up and turned out to be one they knew: the same Ms. David who'd started Abby out her first year at Squaw and who'd made such a fuss over what a natural she was.

So there were a lot of "How are you?"s and "What have you been doing?"s and questions about whether she and Paige would be having lessons again that year. So much talk that Abby had almost forgotten to be nervous by the time she and Paige finally were left alone to head out toward the nearest lift. But sure enough, the minute they were by themselves, Paige grabbed Abby's arm and pulled her to a stop. Shifting her skis and poles around to get her right hand free, Paige reached into her jacket pocket and pulled out a big piece of heavy white cloth—the Plump Jack's napkin. "Okay," she demanded. "Let's see what you can find out."

Abby tried to argue. Her first argument was, why? "What good is it going to do? I mean, even if we find out what run those guys are going to be on today and we go there, what makes you think we're going to . . . I mean, that they're going to . . . The thing is, Paige, what makes you think those guys will be interested in us?"

Paige was indignant. "Why shouldn't they be interested?"

"I don't know, but it seems to me they might be looking for girls their own age."

"Their own age? What do you mean? I'll bet we're as old as they are, or at least just about. They've got to be teenagers, and so are we."

"We're teenagers?" Abby couldn't help smiling.

"Sure we are," Paige said. "Almost." Abby would be thirteen in March and Paige not until May.

"Well, teenagers or not—" Abby was beginning when Paige cut her short. Shoving the napkin back into her pocket, Paige turned her back and started to stomp off. Abby hurried after her. "All right," she said as she caught up. "I'll try. I didn't say I wouldn't try. But . . ." She stopped, looking around at the crowds of people scurrying past in every direction, most of them carrying skis or snowboards. "I'll have to put my skis down somewhere so I can take off my gloves and hold it in both hands and . . ."

Paige nodded. "Oh yeah, right," she said. And then, after a moment's thought, "Follow me."

Back at the lodge in the ladies' restroom, Paige pulled the Plump Jack's napkin out of her pocket and was about to hand it to Abby when two women walked in . . . and then another one . . . and then two more. So finally Abby wound up trying to do the Magic Nation thing in one of the toilet booths while Paige waited right outside. While ski-booted strangers stomped in and out of the booths on each side of Abby, Paige thumped impatiently on the door, whispering, "What's happening? What did you see?"

It wasn't that she didn't try. Clutching the napkin in both hands and shutting her eyes, Abby tried as hard as she could to imagine the beginning of the spinning darkness and the growing warmth in her palms. But absolutely nothing happened. The napkin went on feeling smooth and cool, and the only thing Abby managed to see was the darkness behind her closed eyelids. At last she had to give up and open the door to Paige's eager eyes and questions.

"Okay," Paige demanded. "What did you see? Where are they?"

What happened next was the worst quarrel Abby and

Paige had ever had. It began the minute Abby said she didn't see anything.

Paige stared at her in obvious disbelief. "How come?" she demanded. "What's wrong with this napkin?" She shook it in Abby's face. "It's just the kind of thing you said ought to work. You just didn't try."

"Yes, I did," Abby said. "I tried as hard as I could. I did try. I did."

But Paige only curled her lip and nodded knowingly. "I get it," she said. "You didn't try because you weren't interested. The trouble is, we just don't seem to be interested in the same kinds of things anymore. I guess it's just that you're too immature."

When Abby pointed out that she was older by two and a half months, Paige just snorted and said, "Well, in months maybe, but . . ." Paige was staring at Abby's chest as she went on. "Different people mature faster than others, right?" She obviously meant she had more of a figure than Abby did, which wasn't really fair because, as Abby knew, and as Paige knew she knew, Paige wore a padded training bra. The only reason Abby didn't was that Dorcas felt it was an "unnecessary expense for a skinny twelve-year-old." Actually Dorcas had said, "a very slender twelve-year-old," but skinny was what she'd meant.

And what Paige also meant was that Abby wasn't interested in people of the opposite sex, which wasn't true either. It was just that having gone to a girls' school all her life, plus living in a neighborhood that didn't have many kids, Abby hadn't had many experiences where boys were concerned. Except for the ones she'd had with Paige's brothers, none of which were particularly maturing.

The argument wound up with Paige saying, "Well, since some people are so much slower to mature than other people, maybe there's no reason for us to go on being friends." So Abby said—because what else could she say?—"Fine. If that's the way you feel about it, we'll just stop being friends. I guess I'll get a ride to Truckee and get on the first bus going to San Francisco."

But Paige said, "Now you're just being silly. You know my folks would never let you do that. But just remember, as soon as this trip is over, that's it! You'd better—both of us better—start looking for someone else to be best friends with."

So when they got to the Gold Coast lift and Paige got in line, Abby asked if she should go to another lift and Paige said, "No. Of course not. If we did that we'd have to explain it all to my folks tonight and that would wind up being a total mess. So come on. But just remember, we're not speaking."

So that was how the day went, with Paige and Abby riding the lift up at more or less the same time and skiing down more or less together, but being very careful not to say anything to, or even look at, each other—and even sitting on opposite sides of the restaurant when they went for lunch.

For a while Abby was feeling too miserable to really enjoy the skiing, but soon the bright, beautiful day, and the sleek new snow, not too dry and fluffy and not too hard and icy, and the wonderful freedom to swoop and slide and almost fly began to wipe out her bad mood. All except the part of it that concerned Paige.

That night at dinner, which was pizza and salad around

the kitchen table, there was a lot of talk, most of it about skiing. Paige's mom and dad went on and on about how many times they'd done the Olympic Lady of the KT-22 run and how great it was, and Woody talked about what they'd had for lunch at the Children's Center, and Sky, who was using poles for the first time, had a lot to say about his new poles and how much more fun skiing was when you were old enough to use poles. And Paige and Abby mentioned the lifts they'd tried out and how great it was to get back to skiing. And if the two of them didn't say anything at all directly to each other, no one seemed to notice.

The next day was about the same. Abby and Paige got up at the same time in the same room and went through breakfast and the ride to the lifts without saying anything to each other except for absolutely necessary questions and answers such as "Did you see my sunblock?" "Yes, it's in the bathroom." And on that day, just as on the one before, they saw a great many snowboarders, but none of them were the ones Paige was looking for.

After dinner, so as not to spend any more time than necessary alone in the room with Paige, Abby started spending more time with the boys, particularly Sky. They played a bunch of board and card games, and Abby found out that Sky was really a sharp little kid, especially when it came to things that depended on having a good memory. Usually Woody chose to play with his Game Boy, but once or twice he wanted to play board games too, which often caused trouble, like it had the time when Woody won the checkers game they were playing and Abby told him he was a great checkers player—at which point Sky kicked the board over and ran out of the room.

"Dumb kid," Woody said.

When Abby said, "Oh well, most six-year-olds are bad losers," Woody shrugged. "Oh, Sky's an all right loser. What he can't stand is . . ." He stopped and did one of his fiendish grins. "It's all your fault," he said. "What made him so mad was that you said somebody else was great. That's what turned him into a green-eyed monster."

That night when she got into bed, Abby thought over what Woody had said and decided he'd been right. Where Abby was concerned, Sky really could be a "green-eyed monster." Looking across the room to where Paige was sleeping, or pretending to, Abby sighed and thought, Well, at least somebody still likes me.

16

THE NEXT MORNING, the third since Paige and Abby had stopped speaking to each other, the phone rang while everyone was having breakfast. Paige's mom went to answer it, and when she came back she looked worried. "Well," she said. "I guess we have a problem. It seems Ms. David can only be at the Children's Center this morning, so the juniors' afternoon classes will be canceled." She turned to Paige's dad. "I guess we won't be doing Granite Chief today, Sher. I'd better call the Emersons and let them know we won't be joining them."

Abby had heard of the Emersons before. They were some skiing friends who, like the Bordens, were really expert skiers. "Unless . . ." Daphne Borden paused, looking at Paige. "Unless you and Abby think you could handle being in charge of the boys this afternoon. We could be back to take over around four o'clock."

Paige sighed and said she guessed so.

"After they have lunch you could take them to the Papoose area and just keep an eye on them while they practice," Daphne went on. "Would that be all right with you?" she asked Abby.

"Sure," Abby said. "It's okay with me." She looked across the table to where Sky was drinking milk out of his cereal bowl. Over the edge of the bowl his blue eyes were wide, and when he put the bowl down, so was his milky grin. "Sure," Abby said again. "It'll be fun, won't it, Sky?"

"But didn't the weather report say that it might snow today? What happens if it starts to get really stormy?" Paige asked.

"Well, in that case we'll all knock off for the day," Daphne said. "If it starts looking bad just get the boys in out of the cold and wait for us in the center. And we'll all go home and roast marshmallows in the fireplace."

So that was the plan, and as far as Abby was concerned, it sounded okay. Not great, of course, since she and Paige would have to spend the afternoon fooling around with the boys in an almost flat area set aside for beginners. But at least they would be out in the snow, and—who knew?—maybe if they had to work together at babysitting, Paige would forget about the not-speaking thing at least for a while. Abby was feeling fairly optimistic as she and Paige and the boys climbed out of the SUV, waved good-bye to the adults, and headed for the Children's Center.

That morning was more of the same. Abby and Paige rode the same chair lifts, skied down at more or less the same time, and ate lunch at the same café but at different tables. And when Paige finally spoke to her, it was only to say, "Okay. I guess we'd better go pick up the monsters."

After they checked the boys out and got to the Papoose area, a wide easy slope set aside for beginners, everything was all right—for a while. On their way to the top of the slight rise, Sky kept stopping to fuss with his new ski poles. When they finally got to the top, they schussed down not exactly at top downhill speed, but fast enough to make Sky squeal with excitement. But after a while the fact that Woody came down fast—and teased Sky as he went by—began to bother him. "Hey, slowpoke," Woody yelled, "get a move on."

After the third trip down, Sky began to fret. "Let's not ski with them," he said, looking toward Paige and Woody, who were starting to climb again. "There, let's go over there." He was pointing to another fairly flat area.

Abby should have noticed that the slope Sky was pointing to was the end of another run, a longer and steeper one, and that the whole area was crisscrossed with deep tracks where other skiers and snowboarders had come to rapid stops. But no one was in sight at the moment, and in the last few yards the drop was fairly gentle, so . . .

"Okay, Sky," she said, "let's go over there." And that was when the trouble started.

Abby and Sky had barely started poling their way across the area when suddenly someone yelled, "Watch it!" and what looked like a whole army of snowboarders came flying over the nearest ridge. Snowboard riders sailed through the air all around them, kicking up clouds of snow as they landed. Abby was trying to pull Sky back toward the trees when another snowboard rider zoomed into view practically over their heads, landing so close that snow flew all around them. Abby yelled and Sky screamed and for several seconds everything was mass confusion. The two of them were quickly surrounded by a bunch of tall guys in black jackets who were crowding around, pushing each other and asking questions such as "What are you kids doing on this run?" and "Anybody hurt?" and then "No harm done. Let's catch the next lift."

Most of them picked up their boards and stomped off, but two guys, including the one who had almost collided with Abby, were still hanging around. Abby was trying to tell them it was her fault and she was sorry and she shouldn't have let Sky talk her into moving over there from the Papoose area. And then all of a sudden Paige and Woody were there too.

"What happened?" Paige looked and sounded frantic, or else very excited. "Did you guys hurt somebody?"

One of the two snowboarders, a slightly familiar-looking guy with blond hair and a wide funny grin, threw up his hands. "No sir. I mean, no ma'am. Nobody's hurt. Don't shoot."

Paige grinned back and said, "Why not? There's so many of you snowboard dudes. Don't think anyone would miss one or two."

The other guy laughed and said, "You got something against snowboarders?"

And Paige said, "No, I guess not. At least not as long as they don't land on my little brother."

The shorter guy, the one with a bunch of curly hair hanging out from under his helmet, asked Abby, "What about you? Do you hate snowboarders too?"

And Abby said no, she didn't, and before long they'd all

131

moved to the far side of the run, near the trees, and the two guys, whose names turned out to be Alex and Pablo, were showing Abby and Paige how their feet went on the board and what they did with their bodies to control their speed and direction. Actually they didn't say much that Abby and Paige hadn't heard before, but you'd never know it from the things Paige was saying. Things like "And then what do you do?" and "Really? I never knew that."

Paige was making it obvious that she was very interested, either in snowboarding or possibly in certain people who did it. She asked a lot of questions about what board and boots were the best and how long it took to learn if you already were an expert skier. "Like," she told the two guys, "Abby and I have been skiing since were were rugrats. We were thinking of doing the Fingers today if we hadn't been drafted as babysitters."

The snowboard dudes seemed impressed and surprised, and so was Abby. Surprised, anyway. Only top-level skiers did the Fingers.

"Way to go," the guy named Alex said. "But boarding uses a whole different set of skills. It does help though to have been a skier. Did you know you can take snowboarding lessons right here at the center?"

Then Paige asked about where and how to sign up for lessons, and the other guy, Pablo, started answering her questions. The whole conversation couldn't have been going on more than fifteen minutes when Woody said, "Hey. Where's the midget?" It wasn't until then that anybody noticed that Sky had disappeared.

At first no one was too worried. "He probably had to go to the bathroom and went back to the center," Paige said, and Abby said she'd go see. "You can stay here in case he comes back from somewhere else," she told Paige. And Paige said, "Okay, I'll stay here," which was obviously exactly what she wanted to do. She was still talking to Alex and Pablo as Abby and Woody started for the center.

When they got there Woody went to look in the men's restroom while Abby checked out the café. But Sky wasn't in either place. When they went out of the warm building into the thin cold air, Abby noticed that the clouds that had been drifting around all morning seemed to be getting darker and thicker. And just as she was looking up at the solid gray sky, heavy white flakes began drifting down, slanting sideways in the sharpening wind.

While she was looking up at the threatening sky and thinking about Sky out there somewhere all by himself, and maybe lonely and cold, Abby found herself remembering the kind of warning she'd felt when he'd been captured by Ludmilla. Something like a reflection of the terror he'd been feeling right at that moment. But when she closed her eyes and tried to open her mind to Sky and whatever he was feeling right then, nothing happened. At least nothing for several seconds, and when she did feel, or imagine she felt, a surge of reflected emotion, it wasn't what she'd expected. Not at all like the fright she'd felt outside Ludmilla's kitchen, the quick flash that burned across her mind was more like resentment. Like some sort of "it's your fault" accusation that flickered just once and was gone. Even though she went on trying, there was nothing more.

And then Woody, who'd gone on ahead, yelled, "Hey, come on," and she followed him through the thickening snowfall back to the edge of the woods where Paige and the snowboarders were waiting.

"He wasn't there?" Paige asked, and when Abby shook her head, she said, "Where could he be? Why would he just disappear like that?"

Abby had no answer to the *where* question, but she was beginning to have an awful feeling that she knew something about the *why*. Not for sure, but just maybe, the *why* might be related to why Sky had kicked the checkerboard over and run to his room when she'd paid too much attention to Woody. Only this time it might have been the snowboarders instead of Woody who had turned Sky into a green-eyed monster. But even if that did explain the *why* of it, there was nothing she could feel or see that would explain *where* he might have gone.

A sudden gust of wind raced through the trees that bordered the run, shaking the branches so that here and there heavy clumps of snow broke loose and tumbled to the ground. Abby was staring into the wooded area when she suddenly noticed that the rest of them, Paige and Woody and the two snowboard guys, were doing the same thing.

"Yeah," Alex said. "Where else could he have gotten out of sight so quickly?" And then all five of them shoved off toward the patch of forest. Once into the grove Paige and Abby started calling, "Sky. Skyler! Where are you?" And then they were all calling as they split up and moved farther in among the trees.

A few minutes had passed, ten or even more, before Alex yelled, "Hey. Come here. Everybody come here." Following the sound of his voice, they found him holding up some kid-sized skis and poles. "Are these his?" Alex asked, and grabbing them away from him, Abby demanded, "Where did you find them?"

"Right there." Alex pointed. "The skis and the poles too were right there, leaning against that stump. So he must have left them here, and then . . . what?"

They looked around. The place where the skis had been found was near the end of a deep grove of old-growth pine trees that had been left standing to divide two ski runs. Just beyond the stump, the forest ended as the two runs met and leveled out. So since Sky had come this far and left his gear, it looked as if he might have been headed down the path that led to the center. But Abby and Woody had just been there to look for him—and he wasn't there.

"Maybe he's hiding," Abby said. "I think he might have been angry because no one was paying any attention to him, so maybe he just went off and hid somewhere."

They all looked at Abby, Paige and Woody nodding in agreement, and Alex and Pablo looking surprised and puzzled. "Okay," Alex said. "Let's find him." He started off peeking behind every tree and calling, "Come out, come out, wherever you are. Everybody home free."

The rest of them looked too, spreading out among the trees, where now the snow was sifting down steadily between the already heavily laden branches. But there was no sign of Sky anywhere. When they were all back at the stump where they'd found the skis, Paige said, "I'm getting worried. I think we'd better go back to the center and get some help."

They had almost reached the building when Abby noticed two shadowy figures moving toward them through the swirling snow—two figures that quickly materialized into Paige's mom and dad. Paige gasped and started toward them, shouting, "Mom. Dad. We've lost Sky."

17

WHEN PAIGE'S PARENTS arrived on the scene, a lot of questions were quickly asked and answered. The first questions were about where everyone had been and what they'd been doing when Sky disappeared. Paige and Abby answered everything they could, and Pablo and Alex agreed with them. They explained how there had nearly been a collision and how the snowboarders had come back to be sure everyone was okay. And how they had then started talking about snowboarding. "And that must have been when Sky wandered off," Paige said, "while we were all talking."

"But he didn't tell anyone that he was leaving and nobody saw him go?" Daphne Borden asked, and they all agreed that they hadn't. For a while everyone was talking at once until Sher Borden, who was good at getting people to take turns and answer the exact questions that had been asked, took charge.

When they got to questions about what should be done next, they quickly decided that there was no use going back to search the narrow grove where they'd found Sky's skis, because all five of them, Paige and Abby and Woody and the snowboarders, had been over every inch of the area, and he just wasn't there. But where else could he be? Then Sher went into the center to call the ski patrol.

Once they were all inside the center, Alex looked at the clock and said he and Pablo had to go because his parents were expecting them. But before they left, they gave Daphne their phone number and took the Bordens' so they could find out what happened to Sky. "I'll bet the ski patrol will find him right away," Alex said before he and Pablo picked up their gear and disappeared into the snow.

The rest of them, Daphne and Paige and Woody and Abby, waited in the lobby just outside the booth where Sher was calling. Daphne kept saying things such as "Don't worry. The ski patrol will know just what to do. Don't worry." But her face said something very different and much more frightening.

Abby wandered away to one of the front windows. Rubbing at the mist, she stared out into what was now a blinding swirl of snow. Without even planning to, she found herself concentrating, trying again to sense something, anything at all, about what Sky was thinking and feeling. But nothing was there. No fright or anger or anything else except after a while a relaxed drowsiness. Suddenly remembering something she'd read about how a person about to freeze to death sinks into a kind of dreamlike escape from the cold and pain, Abby knew she had to do something—anything—even if she was almost sure it wouldn't work. She whirled around and ran across the lobby. When she found Paige waiting outside the office where her father was still talking on the phone, Abby hurried to her.

"Where are his skis?" she asked. "What did you do with them?"

Paige didn't need to ask why. Instead she jumped up and headed for the entrance, pushing Abby ahead of her. "Out here," she said. "On the rack. I left them on the rack."

As Paige shoved the two little kid–sized ski poles into Abby's hands, her big eyes looked strangely changed, puckered with worry and fear. This time what she said was not an order. Not "Okay. Do it." Instead she only whispered, "Can you? Will it work?"

"I don't know," Abby whispered back. Doubts flooded her mind. She wasn't sure of anything. How could she be? Sometimes she wasn't sure if it had ever really worked, and she knew for certain it hadn't lately. But she had to try. Clutching the hand grips at the tops of both poles in her hands and closing her eyes, she had hardly started to reach for the warmth and spinning lights when suddenly they were there.

The pole grips had turned from cold to warm to almost hot, and the feeling was once again of relaxed drowsiness— not of freezing cold, and not of fear. Not at all like the terror of Ludmilla's kitchen. The whirling lights were quickly forming into colorless patterns of white and gray and black, like scenes from an old movie. Dark shapes floated together to form what seemed to be the back of a chair upholstered in dark leather. Or the seat of a car? And behind and above the seat was a glassy rectangle that looked like a car window. Beyond the window, a drift of falling snow—and beyond that, darkness and freezing cold.

Opening her eyes and staring into Paige's, Abby whispered, "In a car? Could he be in your car?"

"In our car?" Paige was surprised, amazed, and then suddenly triumphant. "Yes. That's it for sure. He just walked to the parking lot. It's a long way, but Sky could walk farther than that if he was mad enough." She laughed out loud. "That's just what he would do. I'm sure of it."

"But how could he get in?" Abby asked. "Doesn't your dad lock it?"

"Oh sure. But we all know how to get in. See, there's this little emergency key case inside the back fender. Dad taught us all how to open it and get out the key. So he probably just got in the car, and there are all those car blankets he could wrap up in to stay warm. That's it, Abby! You did it!" Grabbing Abby's arm, she pulled her through the door. "Come on. Hurry. We have to tell Dad."

They found Sher and Daphne and Woody peering out through the front entrance. "They're coming," Paige's dad said. "The ski patrol will be here any minute. Don't worry. I'm sure the patrol . . ." Suddenly registering the expressions on the girls' faces, he stopped. "What is it? What happened?"

"Dad," Paige began. "Abby thinks . . ." Glancing at Abby, she started over. "We think—we just got this idea that Sky might have gone to the car. He knows where it is and how to get in. And he could have been almost there before it started to snow very much. Don't you . . ."

Before Paige even finished, Sher Borden had started to

grin. "Yes. Of course. You must be right. That's just what—"

But at that very minute, three men in uniform entered the room. The ski patrol. Glancing around, they headed directly for the Bordens.

"Thank you so much," Sher Borden was saying as they shook hands. "But we may have solved the mystery. It just occurred to the girls that our little boy must have gone to our car. It's just the kind of thing he might do."

"Where is the car, sir?" the tallest patrolman interrupted.

"In the preferred parking lot. Top level."

The patrolmen looked at each other and one of them said, "That's quite a way for a six-year-old to walk."

All the Bordens nodded, but they nodded harder when Paige broke in, saying, "Not for Skyler. He knows the whole area really well, and he's pretty tough for a six-year-old."

"Well," the tall patrolman said. "Why don't we go check it out? Come on. All of you. There's room in the van."

The parking lot was almost empty, and sitting there almost by itself, the Bordens' big snow-covered SUV looked like an igloo. The van had barely slid to a stop when Sher jumped out and clicked open the locks. He slid back the side door and disappeared inside—but by the time the rest of them reached the SUV, he was climbing back out, shaking his head. "He's not here," he said. "Sky isn't here."

Daphne Borden drove Paige and Woody and Abby back to the cabin while her husband went with the ski patrol to continue looking for Sky. The words that kept going through Abby's head were, "To look where? Where could he possibly have gone?" It was Paige who said it out loud.

"Where will they look, Mom? Where could he be?"

Daphne shook her head. Her voice sounded stiff and hoarse as she said, "They'll look first in the center again, I think. The people in the office said he couldn't have come in without being noticed but . . ." She paused and then went on, trying to make what she said sound like the normal way a Borden said such things. "But they don't know . . . our Sky." Her voice cracked halfway through.

"Yeah," Paige agreed quickly. "They sure don't. He probably sneaked in without anybody seeing him and hid someplace. In a closet or something like that."

It was Woody who asked the question they were all thinking but not saying: "But if he's not at the center, where is he?"

No one answered. No one said, "Somewhere out in the storm."

When they got to the Bordens' cabin, Daphne made hot chocolate and insisted that they all drink at least a little. So they tried, but when Daphne left to take Woody to his room, Paige put down her cup and left the kitchen. And so did Abby.

Back in their room, Abby sat on the window seat and stared into almost horizontal currents of windblown snow. The short winter day was over, and beyond the windows' light the forest was endlessly deep and dark. Crouching there, wrapped in blankets and lonely misery, Abby wasn't expecting Paige to join her. In fact, she didn't expect Paige to speak to her ever again. Not now. Not after she had made such a terrible mistake and gotten everyone's hopes up for no reason at all.

But then suddenly Paige was sitting beside her, and as Abby stared in surprise, she said, "I guess you were right when you said it wasn't working anymore. The Magic Nation thing."

Abby swallowed hard before she could answer. "I guess not. My mom said most people stop being able to do it when they grow up. And I thought that had happened to me. But . . ."

"But what?" Paige asked.

Abby's voice tightened as she went on. "But I *did* think I saw a car. I was sure I did. The inside of a car. I wouldn't have told you so if I didn't."

Paige's nod was slow and thoughtful. "I know. I saw how you looked when Dad said Sky wasn't in our car. I was watching you and I could tell. I know you really thought you saw him there."

Abby's throat tightened and her eyes began to burn, and when Paige leaned against her shoulder, sniffing and wiping her eyes, Abby began to cry too. They cried together for a long time while outside the window the swirling snow and howling wind went on and on. At last, without saying anything more, they both got up and went to their beds.

To bed but, for Abby, not to sleep. Staring into the darkness, she continued to go over and over everything that had happened. She had been so sure about the car. How could it have turned out to be so wrong? It had seemed so clear and distinct, but maybe she hadn't looked carefully enough and had jumped to the wrong conclusion. That must have been it. She just hadn't waited to look carefully enough. If only . . . Suddenly she got out of bed and tip-toed out of the room and down the hall. She opened the door to the boys' room very quietly, and in the soft glow of a night-light, she passed Sky's empty bed and the one in which Woody was fast asleep.

Inside the big closet, Abby closed the door before she turned on the light. She knew what she was looking for and where it would be. Just inside the door there were two hooks where the boys hung their pajamas. The higher one, Woody's, was empty, but a small pair of Spider-Man paja-mas still dangled from the lower hook. Clutching Sky's pj's in both arms, Abby closed her eyes and waited.

Once again the warmth was swift and strong, and the spinning shapes formed even more quickly than before. And there again was what had to be the interior of a car—seats covered with dark leather, and, all around, the glassy gleam of windows. This time she could even hear the throbbing hum of a motor and feel a slight sensation of motion. The car was moving, and . . . lying across a rear seat was a lumpy bundle that ended in a familiar tousle of dark blond hair. Abby gasped in amazement and for a hopeful moment she wondered if they'd found him and he was on his way home in the ski patrol's van. But then she knew that couldn't be true, because they would have called immediately if he'd been found. So what she was seeing was just another trick of her imagination, some kind of cruel meaningless deception. Dropping the pajamas, she ran back to bed.

18

SOME TIME LATER Abby woke up to a series of startling sounds. There were footsteps on the stairs—running footsteps—and then a voice calling. Daphne's voice, she realized, calling, "Girls. Girls, wake up. Someone found Sky. He's all right."

Holding a cell phone in one hand, Daphne Borden threw open the door and dashed into the room as Abby and Paige, still only half awake, staggered toward her.

"Where? Where is he? Who found him? Did someone call?" The questions tumbled over each other, and Daphne's answers did too. "He's on his way here. A man named"—she stopped to glance at a piece of paper—"named Jackson Baker called to say that they'd found Sky. Then Sky got on the phone and he said, 'I'm okay,

Mom. I don't think I'm kidnapped. He says he's taking me home.' " Daphne paused again and then caught her breath in a way that sounded almost like a sob. Shaking her head, she added uncertainly, "Mr. Baker asked for our address and when I told him, he repeated it and I could hear Sky in the background saying, 'I told you so.' So I guess they're on their way here from . . ." Her voice trailed away to an uncertain "from Truckee."

"From Truckee?" Paige and Abby repeated in unison. And then Woody, who had just stumbled into the room, made it into a question. "How did Sky get all the way to Truckee?"

"I don't know. Mr. Baker didn't say. He was calling from his car. He said the snow on the road is very bad now but they're following a snowplow and they'll be here as soon as possible."

"And Dad? Does Dad know?" Paige asked.

"Yes. I called him. They were searching in the forest way out past the Far East Express. But now he's on his way here with the ski patrol. Put on your robes and come downstairs. It won't be long now."

It wasn't really long but it seemed like forever. A forever of sitting around the kitchen table wondering how in the world Sky had gotten to Truckee and watching Woody run to the window every few minutes and come back shaking his head.

Mr. Borden and the ski patrol guys arrived first, their van sliding and slipping up the snowy driveway. But while they were still taking off their coats in the snow porch, there was the clanking sound of another car with chained tires coming up the driveway. A few seconds later Sky dashed into the kitchen. Daphne ran to grab him up and then all the Bordens and Abby too were around him, patting his head and back while he buried his face against his mother's shoulder.

There were other voices then, men's voices, and when Abby turned around, a stranger was shaking hands with the patrolmen and introducing himself. "The name is Baker," he was saying. "Jackson Baker."

Daphne sat Sky down on the edge of the kitchen counter while everyone said hello to Jackson Baker and started thanking him for finding Sky and bringing him home.

"Where on earth did you find him?" Daphne asked.

The guy named Jackson grinned. "On the backseat of our car. We—my wife and I—had no idea he was there and then just as we were about to pull into our driveway he started talking. Really gave us a start."

Suddenly everyone was looking at Sky. "Skyler?" Sher Borden said, and that one word was a question. A very big question.

"Okay," Sky said. "I ran away because I was mad at them." He pointed to Abby and Paige. "I was just going to go to the center but then I saw *them* going there. . . ." This time he pointed to Abby and then to Woody. "I saw them coming so I went the other way. And then it was starting to snow and I was cold so I went all the way to *our* car." Sky emphasized the word *our.*

Abby and Paige exchanged significant glances.

"Only when I got there I couldn't get the key out." Sky looked at his father as he went on. "I know how to do it, Dad. I remembered how. Only there was so much ice inside the bumper. I tried and tried and I couldn't get the key out. It was cold and snowing and then I saw a guy coming skiing really fast."

Sitting on the edge of the counter, Sky pantomimed someone doing speedy cross-country skiing. "His car was near ours and he opened the door and reached in and then he went away fast. Real fast. And then . . ." Sky stopped talking, squinted his eyes, and nodded his head, making an expression that said something like "And then I got a good idea."

"Then I went over and tried and I was right." He grinned at Mr. Baker. "You forgot to click your door locker. So I got inside and sat in the backseat. But I wasn't much warmer until I found a big sleeping bag right there on the floor. And then . . ." He paused and then went on sheepishly. "And then I guess I went to sleep."

They all looked around, giving each other "Oh, I get it" expressions, but Sky wasn't finished. "And when I woke up I was riding in a car with a stranger, like Mom says not to. With *two* strangers." Sky shrugged and grinned. "I was kind of scared, I guess. But when I asked them if I was kidnapped, the lady kidnapper screamed, and he"—Sky pointed at Mr. Baker—"he stopped the car so fast I rolled off the seat."

After everyone stopped laughing, Mr. Baker told about how he and his wife had been skiing and it wasn't until they came back to the village and started to go to a restaurant that he realized he'd left his wallet in his car. So he went to get it. "And I must have forgotten to lock the car. By the time we'd finished eating," he said, "the storm was so bad we decided to pack it in and go back to Truckee as fast as we could." He grinned. "And then, just as we got there, we discovered we had a stowaway."

It was very late, maybe almost midnight, when Abby and Paige were back on the window seat, staring out at the storm—and talking and talking and talking. They laughed a lot too, especially at first while they were going over everything that had happened. Things such as how scared the Bakers must have been when a mysterious voice came out of the darkness at the back of their car. And the way Sky politely asked them if he was kidnapped.

But when the talking finally stopped, they went on sitting there—thinking. At least that's what Abby was doing, and she knew that Paige was too. And she was afraid she also knew exactly what Paige was thinking about. But maybe not. Maybe Paige was just remembering how she'd felt when it had looked as if Sky was lost in the storm and maybe frozen to death, and at the same time remembering how often she'd said she would like to wring his neck.

Abby was pretty sure she did know what Paige was thinking, but just to be sure, she said, "I guess you were pretty glad to have Sky back, even though he's a monster sometimes. Is that what you were thinking?"

Paige nodded. "Yeah. I thought about that for a while." She grinned at Abby. "I even told myself to remember how I felt when I thought he was dead the next time I'm about to strangle him."

Abby grinned back and swallowed a sigh of relief. But the relief didn't last long, because Paige went right on talking and what she said next was "But that's not what I'm into right now. What I'm thinking right now is . . ." She turned to give Abby one of her neon-lit, super-focused stares. "What I'm thinking right now is, *you haven't outgrown it after all.* You did it again. Didn't you?"

Abby sighed and nodded. "I guess so."

"What do you mean you guess so? You saw that Sky was in that car."

"I saw a car. At first I thought it was your car, and then when he wasn't there, I thought I had just been fooling myself. That I must have made it all up."

Paige shrugged and said, "Humph! The insides of cars look pretty much alike, particularly when it's so dark. So thinking it was our car when it was really that Baker guy's doesn't mean anything. It doesn't mean your Magic Nation thing wasn't working. Does it?"

"No, I guess not, and then when I tried again . . ." Overwhelmed by the sudden memory of what she had seen, Abby fell silent.

"When you tried again? When did you try again?"

"Last night. After you went to sleep, I went to the boys' room and I held Sky's pajamas and I saw him in a car again—only this time the car was moving. I could even feel the motion and hear the motor. But I didn't believe it. I was sure it was fooling me again, and I was so frightened, and angry too. Like my imagination was playing tricks on me or something. So I came back to bed and the next thing I knew your mother was calling us and . . ." Abby hushed again, thinking, *So it was right. I did see it right.*

"Y-e-a-h!" Paige drawled the word out long enough for it to mean a lot of important things. "So that *proves* you can still do it."

Abby eyed Paige warily, wondering what might be coming next. Wondering, for instance, if Paige had gotten around to returning the Plump Jack's napkin, or if she might pull it out any minute and demand that Abby make another try at locating Alex and Pablo.

Paige was grinning slyly, and then as if she'd been reading Abby's mind, she said, "Don't worry. I don't have that napkin anymore. I gave it to Mom and told her I'd carried it out of the restaurant by mistake, and she said she'd take it back." The grin faded and Paige went on. "I guess it's just that you were right when you said it only worked about something important."

Abby looked up quickly—hopefully.

"Not that meeting Alex and Pablo wasn't important," Paige went on quickly, "but I guess compared to finding Sky . . ." She shrugged.

"That's right," Abby put in, feeling somewhat relieved. "That's what I think. It worked this time because it was important."

Paige was nodding as she stood up, readjusted her blankets, and headed back to bed. She was almost there when she turned back and said, "So now what we have to do is look for some *really important* crimes to investigate."

19

BREAKFAST THE NEXT morning was . . . well . . . different. The wind had died away and the snow had stopped except for the large clumps that now and then fell with a thud from the heavily loaded branches of nearby trees. Everyone talked about the storm, and how much better the weather was now, and whether they would have to wait for the next snowplow to go by before they tried to drive to the village. But between the short bursts of weather talk, there were long quiet spaces. Times when everybody, Sher and Daphne as well as the kids, just looked at each other, but mostly at Sky, without saying much. Nobody mentioned anything about Sky's getting lost and then found again. At least not out loud. It was as if it had somehow become a forbidden subject.

Sky was quieter than usual too. He fixed himself a bowl of cereal and some orange juice without asking for help, and whenever he caught someone looking at him, he turned his head away, hiding his eyes under his long eyelashes.

"It's how he acts when he's been punished," Abby whispered to Paige. "Or when he thinks he's going to be."

"Yeah," Paige whispered back. "Or else knows he *ought* to be. Scaring everybody half to death the way he did." And then she slowly repeated, "Scaring—*everybody*."

She jumped up suddenly and rushed across the room to where her mother was loading the dishwasher. Abby followed in time to hear her say, "Mom. Do you have the phone number for where Alex and Pablo are staying? We told them we'd let them know what—"

"I know. I know." Paige's mom patted her shoulder. "I called them before you woke up. They were very happy to hear Sky was all right." And then, after a moment, she said, "They were just on their way out, so there's no point in calling again."

"Yeah. Okay. Okay." Paige sighed, shrugged, and went back to her breakfast.

Then Daphne told Abby that she'd called her mother too. "I thought she might be worried because of the storm. She said she had been concerned and she thanked me for letting her know we're all fine."

So Abby went back to cleaning up, and as soon as the snowplow went past and Sher finished using the blower on the driveway, they all headed for the car. But then, while they were gathering up their gear, Sher came in and said, "Don't forget your ice skates, girls." And when Paige asked why, he said, "Just do as I tell you. The answer to *why* will come as soon as we get this show on the road."

Even before Paige gave her an excited flick of the eyes, Abby was close to guessing. But it wasn't until the whole family and all their equipment had been packed into the SUV that she found out her guess was a good one.

"Okay, troops," Paige's dad said as they started down the drive, "Daphne and I have decided that since we're leaving tomorrow, it would be fun to do something a little different today. Like spending the whole day at High Camp. So, where we're headed right now is straight to the Cable Car. Okay? Forward! March!"

The boys cheered, and Abby, who had been to High Camp just once before, felt like cheering too. At High Camp, a special development two thousand feet above the valley floor, there were three restaurants, an ice-skating rink, a swimming pool, tennis courts, and a lot of good ski runs, including some that were okay for little kids like Woody and Sky. The Cable Car ride all by itself was a big thrill, and a visit to High Camp's ice-skating rink was an exciting prospect for a person who, after only a few tries, thought that someday she might love ice-skating almost as much as skiing.

From the moment the Cable Car began to move, skimming smoothly up high above the snowy mountainside, Abby's premonition that it was going to be an extraordinary day got stronger and more certain. And sure enough, one surprise seemed to follow another. One of the first ones was when Daphne announced that she and Sher would go to the beginner's slope to help the boys, instead of sending Abby and Paige to do it—which meant that Abby and Paige could go to the rink immediately. And once out on the ice, Abby was again surprised at how well she was able not only to get around the rink without falling, but also to swoop and glide, almost as if she'd done it all her life.

When noon came, there was a great lunch at a table where you could see all the way down to Lake Tahoe, and afterward the whole family went out to the slopes again. Having their parents watching and admiring them made Woody and Sky do a lot more skiing and a lot less arguing. And later, when they all moved to a steeper slope, Paige and Abby got to show how much they'd improved. The skiing was fantastic, and all during the day everybody did a lot of talking. Not just about skiing and skating, but also about things that had happened at school and at work, and even on the tennis court. A lot of important things got said, but for some reason, not a word about what had happened just the night before did, which made Abby wonder uneasily if what was being put off for the future was a serious discussion about who was to blame for losing Sky.

But Paige didn't seem to be worried at all. In fact she kept saying how it was an absolutely insane day. And then, just as they were about to leave, something happened that made it seem even more so. At least right at first.

Abby and all five of the Bordens were waiting for the next Cable Car down to the valley floor when Abby noticed a big bunch of snowboarders ahead of them in the line. Because of their helmets, it wasn't easy to tell one snowboarder from another, but before long, Abby recognized two of them: Alex by his lanky height and sharp outfit, and Pablo by the way he tossed his head back when he laughed.

Abby saw them first, but when she poked Paige and

pointed, it was Paige who yelled and waved. "Hey, Alex," she shouted. "Hi, Pablo."

They came over then, both of them, and said hi to everyone, especially to Sky. At first Sky looked embarrassed, almost resentful. But when the guys kept talking to him, he began to loosen up.

"Hey, dude. Good to see you," Pablo said. "We sure were glad when your mom called this morning and said they'd found you."

"Yeah, right," Alex said. "We heard you decided to take a little trip to Truckee. Nice going, bro."

"No." Sky shook his head firmly. "I didn't *decide* to. I was kidnapped. Only they changed their minds and brought me back." When everyone laughed, Sky's wobbly grin made it clear that he'd expected them to.

Having a chance to talk to Alex and Pablo was a plus for more reasons than one. For one thing, it seemed to make it possible again for everybody to talk about Sky's disappearance in a way that didn't make anyone wonder who was going to get blamed for letting it happen.

But then came a big minus. When the line began to move, Alex and Pablo said good-bye and went back to their snowboard friends, some of whom you could tell, if you looked closely, were girls. Teenage girls, like Abby and Paige were just about to be, but probably a couple of years more mature. And all of whom seemed to be very friendly with Alex and Pablo.

On the Cable Car and then in the SUV Paige was unusually quiet. Abby was pretty sure she knew why, and she wished there was something she could say that would cheer Paige up. But there wasn't much that could be said.

The problem was, Abby thought, it looked as if she'd been right about Alex and Pablo being interested in older women. She wished she hadn't been right, but it looked as if it were true.

They were almost home when Abby leaned across to Paige and whispered, "We'll probably see them again next year, and by then we'll be teenagers too."

But Paige only gave her a blank stare and said, "What are you talking about? I don't care what those dudes do. I've got more important things on my mind."

And Abby said, "Oh. Well, that's good then. I'm . . . I'm glad."

And she was glad, at least for the moment. It wasn't until later that she began to wonder just what important things Paige was referring to. But that night on the window seat, when she came right out and asked, Paige would only say she wasn't ready to talk about it yet.

On the trip home to San Francisco, things went a little bit better than they had on the way up. Woody tried the rubber spider thing again. But a rubber spider only works once, and when Abby started treating it like an old friend, he quickly lost interest. Woody and Sky still quarreled about the dividing line between their private spaces, but their arguments weren't as loud and ferocious, as if they were just doing it for old times' sake.

For once the roads were clear all the way down the mountain, they had lunch at Paige's favorite restaurant, and they arrived in the Bay Area a little earlier than usual. And then Abby was running up the front steps of the O'Malley Detective Agency, where, as she was about to discover, there had been another change. A big one.

RIGHT AT FIRST everything at the agency seemed the same as always. The same cluttered office overflowed from the ex-parlor into the ex-dining room, where, at about five-thirty on a Sunday afternoon, no one was there to welcome her home. No big surprise. Private eyes worked when they found a clue—weekend or not. It wasn't until she'd dumped her duffel bag in the hall and gone into the kitchen that she found Dorcas was at home after all. Sitting at the kitchen table, Dorcas and Abby's dad were drinking coffee and listening to old-fashioned music on the radio.

"Abby. You're early." Dorcas jumped up and ran to hug Abby and kiss her on both cheeks. "We didn't hear you come in. Are the Bordens still here?"

"No, they went on home," Abby told her. "Sher was in a

hurry to get some stuff ready for the office tomorrow. Daphne said she'll call you in a little while."

Abby's dad hugged her too and pulled her down to sit beside him. "Well, how did it go, kid?" he asked. "Heard you had quite a snowstorm up there."

So Abby began to tell them about Squaw, and even included an only slightly censored version of what had happened to Sky—of how he had run off because he'd felt he was being ignored and wound up sleeping in someone else's car while they drove all the way to Truckee. To her surprise, her dad and Dorcas seemed to think it was an awfully funny story. And after watching them look at each other and laugh some more, she found it was easier to forget the bad parts, such as the long hours of wondering if Sky was still alive, and how awful it felt to think it was mostly her own fault.

While they were all laughing about Sky asking the Bakers if he was kidnapped, it occurred to Abby that both of them were in an especially good mood, and when she asked, "Hey, what's up? Is something special going on?" the truth about the big change began to come out.

"See?" her mom said to her dad. "What did I tell you about Abby's psychic powers? I told you she'd know immediately."

And before Abby had time to start being resentful about the "powers" thing, her dad put his hand over Dorcas's and said, "I'm sure you're right. But I don't think it would take much psychic power to tell that we're feeling pretty good at the moment." And then to Abby he said, "We were planning to wait until tomorrow to tell you, but since you seem to have guessed—your mom and I are thinking about giving it another try."

And before he had time to go on, without needing to use a bit of psychic power, Abby knew exactly what he would say. They were going to get married again—to each other. Without meaning or planning to, Abby let out a delighted shriek and hugged them both, one at a time and then both at once. The questions came later, but not a lot of them. Nothing like "What made you change your minds?" in case remembering the things they used to fight about might not be a good idea right at the moment.

One answer that came up without any asking was that they had come to an important agreement. A two-way agreement in which Abby's dad had said that Dorcas should go on running the O'Malley Agency, as long as she stopped living in it. "So as soon as we find a house that suits all three of us," Abby's dad said, "we'll buy it and the three of us will move in."

"And Tree will take over here," Dorcas said. "She's delighted. Delighted for us and for herself too. Her new commute—from the kitchen to the parlor—is going to be a bit easier than having to cross the Bay Bridge at rush hour."

There were even plans for the wedding, and Abby would be part of it. "As a witness," Dorcas said, "or it might be fun for you to be my bridesmaid, if you'd rather."

Abby was thrilled and she knew Paige would be too. She couldn't wait to tell her and invite her and all the Bordens to the wedding.

Of course Paige thought the whole thing was "totally insane." In fact she was the one who decided that she would be a bridesmaid too and then came up with lots of important details, such as the pattern for the dresses she and Abby would wear, and the kinds of flowers they would carry in their bouquets.

Dorcas was a little concerned about the cost of all that satin and lace, but Daphne insisted on paying for some of the material. And then, when Tree offered to do the sewing, the expense problem was pretty much solved. It turned out that along with being an excellent secretary and detective (not to mention being insanely gorgeous, which you didn't if she was in earshot), Tree was also an expert seamstress. The way Tree explained it, her parents had insisted she learn to sew as part of her preparation to be a perfect wife for the rich husband she was supposed to marry. And even though she hadn't appreciated the rest of their plan, Tree had discovered that she really liked to sew.

So it wasn't long before Paige and Abby were going directly from school to the agency every day to help by posing for pattern adjustments and doing a little carefully supervised pinning and basting. At least that's what Abby thought they were doing. It wasn't until several days had passed that she discovered what else Paige had been up to.

Abby hadn't suspected a thing until the day the three of them (Dorcas was away on a case) were using the kitchen table to cut out two pairs of satin sleeves. Abby realized that Paige was missing and had been for some time. When she went to investigate, she once again found Paige going through a file in the office, this time in the cabinet where Dorcas kept her new cases.

Instead of answering Abby's "What do you think you're doing?" in a guilty way, Paige slowly put the file she'd been reading back in the drawer, took hold of Abby's arm, and led her to the row of client chairs.

When they were both sitting, Paige said, "Do you know if your mother is working on any murder cases?"

"No, I *don't*." Abby was shocked. "I told you. She doesn't tell me about her cases, at least not any important ones." Abby had no sooner said the word *important* than she began to get the picture—to guess that Paige had been going through the files looking for crimes that were "important" enough for Abby's Magic Nation thing to play a part in solving them.

"Paige," Abby said uneasily. "When people talk to a detective, they expect the things they say to be private. There's probably a law that says so, and you were breaking it. Do you really want to get us sent to jail?"

But Paige only shrugged and said, "Look, Abby. Nobody's going to put us in jail. For one thing we're too young. And that's one reason we're going to be such great detectives. The criminals are going to think that we couldn't possibly know anything, so when we're around they'll just go on saying and doing things that will give them away. And then you'll do one of your Magic Nation things—"

"No. No, I won't." Abby took a deep breath and began to say something that she knew had to be said, even if it meant another quarrel—a quarrel that, this time, probably *would* be the end of being Paige Borden's best friend. "It's *my* Magic Nation and from now on I'm going to be the only one to decide how to use it. And I don't want you to ever mention it again unless I bring it up first. Okay?"

For a long moment she stared into Paige's blue eyes, and as Paige stared back, her eyes widened with astonishment, narrowed with anger, and then, along with her smiling lips, gradually tipped upward. Putting her arm over Abby's shoulder, she said, "Okay, okay! Come on, let's go look at our sleeves."

As soon as the bridesmaid dresses were finished, the two of them went back to spending most of their after-school hours at the Bordens, and Abby discovered that there had been some changes there too. The most important one was that Ludmilla had run away to Beverly Hills to cook for some movie stars. Sky was delighted of course, but Daphne was desperately looking for a new cook. In the meantime meals at the Bordens' were a lot like the ones at Squaw, when it was Every Man for Himself. Abby loaned them some of the quick-'n'-easy recipes she'd collected for Dorcas, and most of the time the Bordens seemed to be enjoying the kitchen experience, even though the results usually weren't all that great.

So as January ended, there were things to look forward to. There would be the wedding, and helping to choose the new house, and in February there would be at least one three-day weekend at Squaw. And even more fabulous—most fabulous of all—there would be living with her mom and dad too in the kind of "normal" family she'd been hoping for, for a long time.

Concerning Paige's promise to forget about looking for an important enough case to make the Magic Nation thing work, who knew? Abby wasn't sure she believed it. And as for what she herself believed, such as whether she'd outgrown the Magic Nation thing, and even whether it had ever been much more than her imagination, she still wasn't entirely sure. But what she did believe was that if something as important as finding Sky ever happened again, she'd probably give it a try.

ABOUT THE AUTHOR

ZILPHA KEATLEY SNYDER has written many popular and award-winning books for young readers, including *The Egypt Game, The Headless Cupid,* and *The Witches of Worm,* all Newbery Honor Books and ALA Notable Books. Her most recent novels were *The Unseen, The Ghosts of Rathburn Park, Spyhole Secrets,* and two novels about Gib Whittaker, *Gib Rides Home* and *Gib and the Gray Ghost,* which were inspired by stories her father told her about his childhood in a Nebraska orphanage.

Zilpha Keatley Snyder lives in Marin County, California.